The Hostage

BOOKS BY DEBORAH HILL

THE KINGSLAND SERIES
This is the House
The House of Kingsley Merrick
The Heir

Also

The Pretender

and

EDITED BY DEBORAH HILL

*Recollections of a Cape Cod Mariner:
Elijah Cobb, 1768–1848*

The Hostage

DEBORAH HILL

NORTH ROAD
PUBLISHING

Copyright © 2016 by Deborah Hill

ISBN: 978-0-9961163-3-6 (softcover)
ISBN: 978-0-9961163-4-3 (epub)
ISBN: 978-0-9961163-5-0 (kindle)

All rights reserved
Published in the United States by
North Road Publishing Corporation

www.northroadpublishing.com

Cover photo credits: (woman) iStockphoto © PeopleImages,
(man) iStockphoto © Juanmonino, (landscape) iStockphoto © Wabunzi.
Image manipulation by RD Studio.

Book design by DesignForBooks.com

French language translation by
Dr. Guerdie Darbouze Joseph, Ph.D.

Dedicated to the Legacy of Samuel Adams

he organized the Revolution

Note from the Author

Though written forty years ago, **The Hostage** was never published. This proved to be fortunate, as my research was flawed. There was no internet then, and such knowledge as I had about the Acadians, the Native Americans, and the convolutions of the French and Indian War came from books at the public library. When I started looking over the manuscript a year or two ago, checking my facts with the internet, a different and much more detailed history emerged around which my characters would have to interact. A lot of work needed to be done if I was going to maintain my reputation as a historically reliable writer.

I rewrote the novel.

History can bog a story down with the speed of light, so I've chosen to bring some salient points to the fore here, in this note, rather than belabor my plot with them. They'll make **The Hostage** more easily understandable. If the reader chooses to move ahead now, no harm is done, but I'd recommend keeping the enclosed map handy.

England had been at war with France off and on for more than 500 years. So it was the same old story when King William's

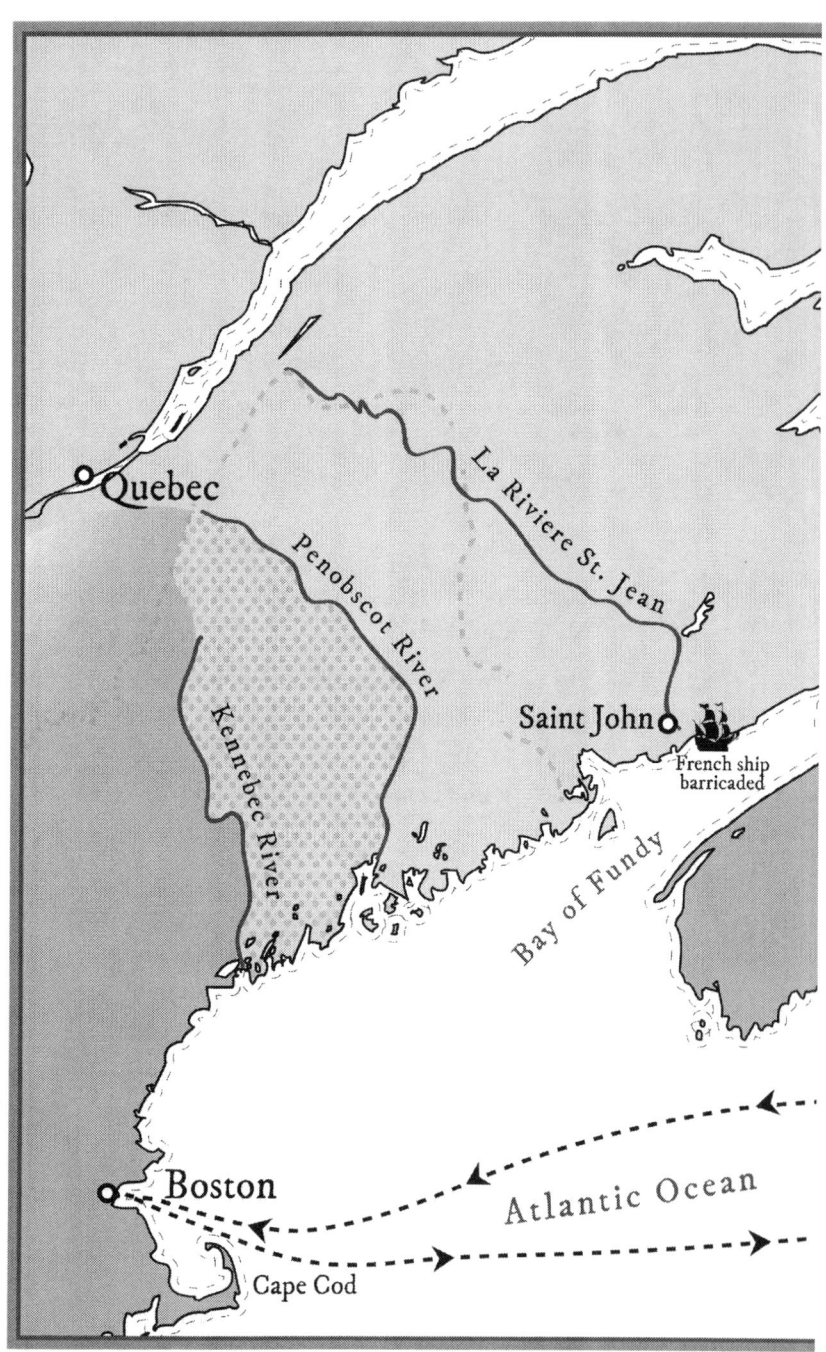

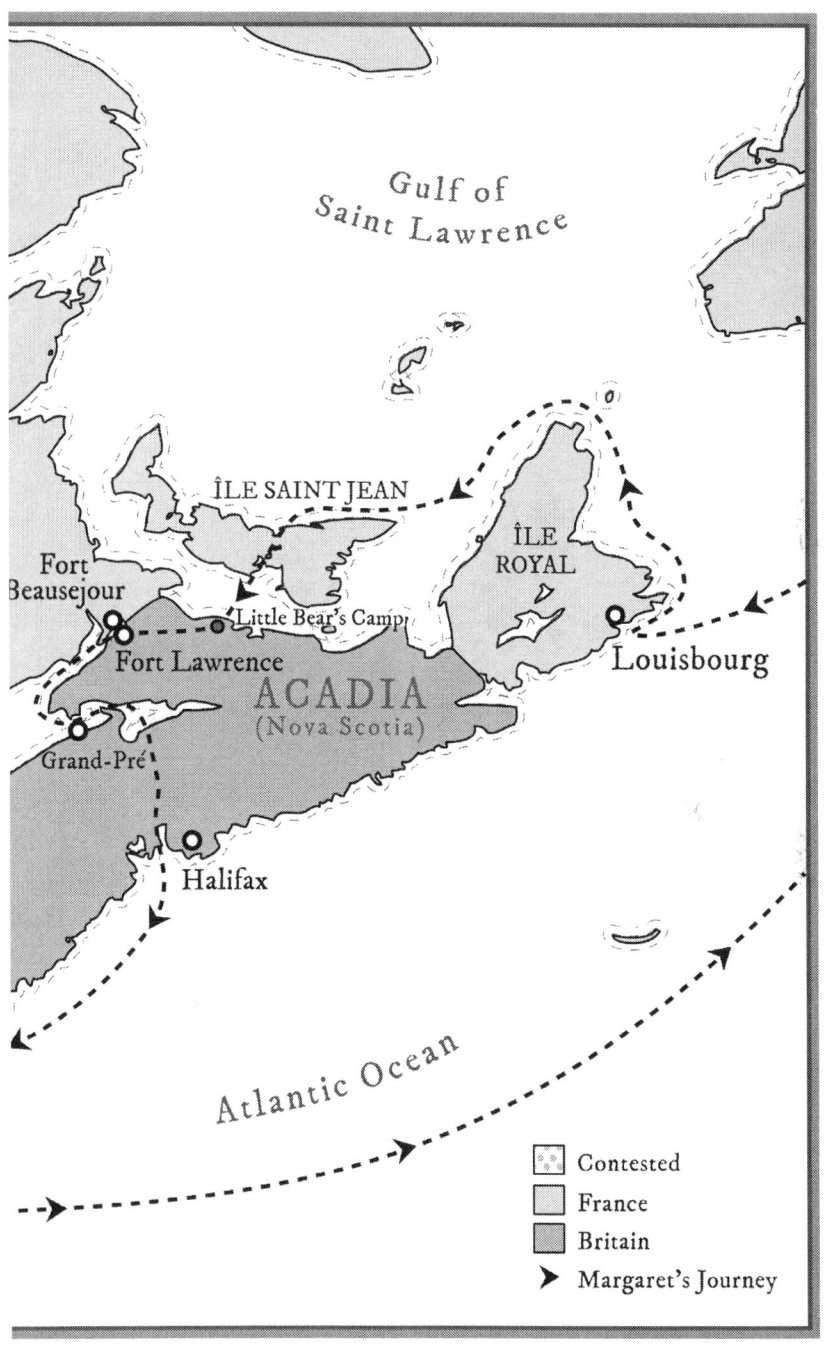

War began in 1688, but this time hostilities took place in the New World as well as Europe. Conflict erupted again in 1703, with Queen Ann's War. This clash concluded in 1713 and, at that time, a portion of France's North American holdings was given to England by treaty—a large peninsula which was immediately renamed Nova Scotia. (The French had called it, and all of their North American territories, Acadia.)

There was a sizeable population of French farmers living there at the time. One hundred families had been imported in 1650 as a sort of colonizing experiment that was never continued, but the families grew and multiplied happily, and seemed not too concerned about being under British control—until—

But I am getting ahead of myself. Returning to 1713 and the treaty, it is important to note that Île Royale, north of Nova Scotia, remained under French control. On it was Fort Louisbourg. If there were going to be more wars, Louisbourg was in a good position to offload French troops and provide safe harbor the French Fleet. The very presence of the fort suggested that the French could retake Acadia/Nova Scotia whenever they felt like it, and contested land in the Maine Territory too.

Meantime, privateering went forward, preying on the English shipping lanes, a constant menace.

When a new war (King George's, in 1744) broke out, 1000 militia men from Massachusetts took the opportunity to sail up to Île Royale and capture the fort. How proud of that victory everyone was despite the high cost of human life, and how low everyone was cast when, by treaty in 1748, Louisbourg was given back to the French.

At that point, the British decided it was time to occupy their territory in Nova Scotia/Acadia. They constructed a fort at Halifax without seeking an accommodation with the local natives.

The French had always honored the Mi'kmaq claim that Acadia was theirs, a gift of the Great One, asking permission when they wished to use the land or even travel across it. The English couldn't be bothered.

Thus began a local war, directed by the priest Jean-Louis LeLoutre and carried out by some Acadians led by Joseph Broussard (Bonsoleil) with the help of the Mi'kmaq. Forts constructed were destroyed, soldiers occasionally captured, tortured and killed. The aim was to discourage British settlement until such time as another treaty returned Nova Scotia to French control.

But it was no use. The French Fort Beausejour was taken in 1754, compromising land access to Louisbourg and Quebec City. Father LeLoutre was captured. The Acadians—now numbering 6000—were deported, the French and the Indians eventually defeated. Finis. End of story.

Meanwhile, the English Exchequer was badly diminished. This most recent war was the last straw, as far as the British citizenry was concerned, and Parliament dared not lay yet another tax on it. Who, then, was going to pay the bill?

Hmmmm. Who were the beneficiaries?

Why, the colonies, of course!

And so, after you've read **The Hostage**, you might want to move on to **The Pretender**, set in 1765, when the colonists discovered that *they* were going to pay the bill. The Stamp Act was, in fact, a prelude to the Revolution, as was the Tea Party in 1773. The leadership of Samuel Adams was covert in the days of the Stamp Act and the Townsend Acts that followed it, but he was no longer working under cover in 1773. The Tea Party was masterminded by him, as well as many subsequent events. Knowing this, it is easier to understand why the inscription at the base of his statue at Faneuil Hall in Boston reads: He Organized the

Revolution. But we know now his involvement didn't start with the Tea Party. Or even with the Stamp Tax. It had begun just as **The Hostage** opens, slowly, slowly leading to that inevitable conclusion when men beat their pruning hooks into swords, and their plowshares into shields, and their wives and sisters and daughters stood beside them . . . .

—Deborah Hill
April, 2017

CHAPTER

1

1755

Boston

Margaret Roberge held the last note of the lullaby and let it fade into a whisper. The receiving room was quiet as everyone in it sighed, then broke into well-modulated applause.

"Oh, she is quite, quite marvelous!" exclaimed Madam Blake.

"Margaret's teacher told me she has perfect pitch," Mama murmured modestly.

Papa leaned forward, the better to engage the Blakes. "She's been singing like a bird since earliest childhood," he bragged.

Her suitor leaped to his feet, his hands pattering as he called, "Huzzah! Huzzah!"

Robert Blake, of the illustrious Summer Street Blakes.

Je le deteste. I detest him, she told herself as she observed the jewels on his fingers flashing in the afternoon sunlight.

Curtseying to his parents, then hers, she took the hand he extended, reseating herself beside him on the settee they shared. Across the hearth were her parents, in front of it were his. The hearth itself was decorated now, in spring-time, with a spray of brilliant forsythia that Mama had brought into the house for forcing, to be ready for a gathering like this one. Robert had asked for and received permission to court the Roberge daughter; his parents were charmed by her, and it was only a matter of time before the fathers would discuss the dowry and an agreement reached that would satisfy all parties. Except Margaret herself.

"I shall tell His Excellency about her," Mrs. Blake declared. She was the daughter of an English aristocrat, a lowly one to be sure, but, in America, any connection to the nobility guaranteed entrée to the governor and his social circle. This entrée also included her husband, Mr. Donald Blake, seated beside her now and doing his best to stay awake.

Papa, of course, could brag about his own noble blood— the earliest Huguenots included aristocrats, among whom was his ancestor. Thus was Margaret a suitable match for the Blakes' second son. In addition, she spoke French, as did many Bostonians of Huguenot descent, and, with her dark hair and eyes, pretty figure, refined manner and proud carriage, she would be a welcome addition to the Blake entourage. Besides which was the possibility that the business interests of both families could be merged. If not now, then later. A truly happy prospect.

Flicking open her fan, Margaret fluttered it decorously. "Not the governor, Madam Blake!" she protested prettily. "His expectations would be too high!"

The desired effect was achieved, causing an effluvium of protests, encouragements, jests and general agreement that such a recital must take place sometime soon. Perhaps at the governor's new mansion in Roxbury, completed a few years ago and completely elegant.

Repartee no longer necessary, Margaret retreated behind a sweet smile, her loathing well hidden. If she were not friendly with Tyler Moore, she'd no doubt be more pleased at the prospect of marrying Robert. Liking your husband was not a requirement

CHAPTER ONE

of matrimony, but when there was another man with whom to compare him....

It was through the family business that she'd first come to know Tyler, five years ago. She'd just turned twelve then, and was considered responsible enough to take advertising copy to the printer.

Tyler was apprenticed to Enoch Wagner, owner of Boston's *Colonial Press*. On that day, when Margaret first ventured out on her own as her father's assistant, he had been setting type for an editorial written by Mr. Wagner. It was a protest against the new treaty between France and England that returned Fort Louisbourg to the French.

"Louisbourg?" she had asked, reading the first page of the Press that was hanging from a line of twine, like laundry. "They gave it back?"

WAR ENDED! The largest headline read.

FORT RETURND.

Tyler's hands had been trembling as he set type for the second page. Young as she was, Margaret understood his distress. She waited patiently for him to acknowledge her so she could ask for Mr. Wagner.

Who was gone for the rest of the morning, Tyler finally told her, drinking at the tavern with all the other men who were enraged by the return of Louisbourg. Only three years ago, Governor Shirley had led 1000 militia up there expressly to take the fort which menaced British and American shipping. After a fairly easy campaign it had been captured, but more than seven hundred Massachusetts men subsequently died while stationed there, either from exposure to the hostile elements so far north, or of disease caused by unsanitary conditions and inadequate diet. Among them was Tyler's own brother.

"That's a truly terrible thing, giving it back," she commiserated. "You have every right to be distressed. I wish I could help."

He continued to set type, but her sympathy had a soothing effect and he became more relaxed. At last he calmed enough to take the Roberge advertisement from her hand.

"Not bad."

"I designed it myself," she announced with pride.

"We've done ads for your company before. Linen goods, as I remember."

"Irish linen. Especially Irish damask."

"Must get a lot of business from the Court Crowd, and the governor's house, too," he remarked. "I imagine they never use anything but damask." Then he asked how it came to be that so young a girl was employed in business, rather than as a maid or nursery attendant—and this had led to other subjects of conversation. Despite the five year age difference between them, they'd both enjoyed their association; recently, more than enjoyed.

Tyler!

Suddenly everyone in the Roberge receiving room was standing, her parents bidding the Blakes unctuous farewells, Robert bowing over her fingertips, softly touching them with his lips.

She suppressed a shudder.

"Let's talk soon," Mr. Blake said to Papa.

"That would be my pleasure," Papa responded. With thanks and exclamations about nothing at all, the Blakes stepped into their carriage, waiting in front of the house. There were few carriages in Boston. Only very wealthy people had them.

Lucy, Mama's neice, peeked from around the kitchen door. "They are gone, I take it. I heard everything. It sounded as though the meeting went well."

She had cared for Margaret always, while Mama—her auntie—worked at Papa's side, attending customers and stocking

CHAPTER ONE

shelves. A virtual member of the family, Lucy knew everything. What a relief to see her now, unimpressed by the Blakes' wealth, but understanding why cultivating them was important.

"I think they really like us," Mama told her.

"What think you, Uncle Roberge?" Lucy asked.

Papa nodded. "I'll call on *le Pére* Blake soon and start negotiations. It's time we got serious."

Margaret's fate was all but sealed, and she knew it. But she had prepared for this moment; the opportunity to make even Robert Blake tolerable was at hand.

"We need to talk about the company before discussing marriage, do we not?" she asked. "Ownership of the company?"

"Let's sit down," Lucy urged quickly. "This may take some time." She knew Margaret's position and was prepared to support it.

Papa sighed. The company—Roberge Imports—had occupied his and Mama's life ever since they married, and Margaret was his only heir.

She wasted no time on the niceties. "I am seventeen years old, Papa. Old enough to marry, and old enough to own the company. You've trained me well, and you'll be right here to supervise me. And hopefully you'll be right here for a long time to come."

Had they been Catholics, they'd have crossed themselves. Mention of death was risky, even more so for Papa, who had been unwell all winter. To speak of it was to court it. They were quiet as they took their places in front of the forsythia.

Into the silence, Lucy remarked, "It's not as though Robert were the oldest son, Uncle."

"That's right," Mama agreed. "He won't inherit the major portion of Blake Enterprises stock. But his position would be greatly improved by bringing Roberge Imports into the fold."

"Well, that's a bit problematic, isn't it? I haven't even so much as hinted that Margaret might own the company outright, before the two of them are wed. And will insist on continuing to own it after they marry."

They thought about it. Could Robert be persuaded to sign a pre-nuptual agreement?

Lucy, fair as were all Mama's Anglo-Saxon family, twirled a flaxen curl. "If you intend to see that the business stays in the family, Uncle, you must turn it over now. But you could offer part of our profit to enlarge Robert's income." She and Margaret had labored over this point at length. "Then Mr. Robert would be better off than before. After all, if you, not Margaret, were to continue owning the company, he'd get nothing."

Father cleared his throat and the women were quiet. "Robert's position would be traditional in all other respects. I hope you realize that, Daughter. Your children would be his. And the house you'd live in and everything in it. His wishes would still be your command. Do you find him agreeable?"

"I think you know he would not be my first choice," Margaret straightened her young shoulders. "But I realize he is suitable."

"He's more than suitable, darling!" Mama exclaimed. "If America ever gets an aristocracy, his family will be part of it, and so will you!"

"You'd be Lady Margaret," Lucy teased. Neither of them were admirers of England's nobility, people who had simply been born into the right family without having to work their way up in the world. They wrinkled their noses in distaste, and, with Mama, waited for the head of the household to come to a decision.

Finally Father sighed. "Mrs. Roberge, I think it sensible for you to take Margaret to Dublin as soon as possible," he said. "You can introduce her, and let everyone know about the new arrangement. And then to London, to meet our suppliers there, too."

He'd said it! Out loud! He'd agreed!

"And I'll be here, Auntie," Lucinda said. "And Cook, too. We'll take good care of Uncle."

"Actually, if both you and Meg were gone, I believe I could make the necessary arrangements with the Blakes more easily," Papa interjected, now committed. "Going to meet our suppliers and producers shows them that I am serious about Meg's being my heir. I can offer the household allowance you mentioned, Lucinda, and I can hint that a merger is not impossible sometime in the future. Margaret might prefer to be at home rather than in the counting house when there are babies coming along."

It was a delicate topic in view of the many miscarriages and stillbirths endured by Mama, but she did not flinch. "You could even propose a date for the wedding, Husband, based on our return."

"Let's get you on your way first, my dear. Then I'll go to Blake unencumbered, as it were."

"It's April now," Mama calculated. "We'd leave Ireland and be in London sometime in June. Set sail for home early in July, return sometime in August."

"Then, if all goes well, the bans might be posted in October," Lucy added.

In unison, the three of them looked at Margaret.

Five months. She'd have to marry in five months. "Very well," she agreed, despite her misgivings. After all, she'd have escaped coverture. Except for the allowance, Robert would have no legal right to her income, nor any say in how she would run the business. Lucy could help at the store—she was good at sales—and if children arrived and lived, there'd be plenty of money to hire nursemaids and nannies. One of those children, in his or her turn, would inherit Roberge Imports and carry the Huguenot tradition on a generation further. It was a worthy goal.

She jumped to her feet and clapped her hands, to cover her reluctance. "Let's make up an advertisement for special orders that

Mama and I can buy and bring back with us when we come. I can run it over to Mr. Wagoner's print shop tomorrow morning."

"I'll get paper and ink right now!" Lucy crowed. "Let's do a circular as well as an ad. I'll post it around town."

"I'll leave you ladies to it," Papa said fondly, and went off to his afternoon rest.

> Roberge Imports will soon be sendng
>   Repersentativs to Ireland,
> To purchase the finest damask, the best linens,
> and wool of the hyest grade, spun and not spun.
>   Order now!
> Delivry in six months time.
>   Persons Intrested
> May Contact the Proprietors
>   at #10 Dock Square

Tyler Moore looked it over, then asked, "Are you one of the repersentatives?"

There was no way to avoid his blazing blue eyes. "Yes."

"How nice for you, visiting Ireland and all."

"That's where the damask industry is. You know that."

"Yes, yes, so you've told me. The Huguenots went there and started up mills like the ones they owned in France. And, of course, you'll visit London, too?"

"How else can I meet the suppliers who order our stuff from Dublin and pay the duties and send it here. Listen, Tyler—he's done it! My father has finally said he will make me owner of Roberge Imports!"

He should have been rejoicing, knowing how much she had hoped for ownership. Instead, he looked into her eyes for a long, miserable moment.

CHAPTER ONE

"In exchange for marrying that ass, Robert Blake."

"Yes."

Anger and hurt swept across his face as he came around the counter. Sweeping on by her, he ripped the "open later" sign off its peg, hung it on the shop's door and slammed it closed.

"I need to talk." The Roberge advertisement forgotten, he led her to the shop's back room, a place they had often visited when the Master wasn't looking.

"Where's Mr. Wagner?"

"Out delivering bills. Back any time, so we cannot dally. I must know how things stand between Blake and you?"

"Father thinks it's time to speak to Mr. Blake. He says he'll take care of the arrangements while Mother and I are gone. When we get back, Robert and I will marry."

"Oh, God!" he cried, turning away, fists clenched. "Is there no way to stop this travesty?"

"Tyler, Tyler," she soothed, taking his arm and turning him back to face her. "I have to marry someone agreeable to my parents, sometime. They'll never let me marry you, so why not a man who can do us some good?" she cajoled. "I'm all but guaranteed entrance to the governor's circle, after all. I might be able to learn things your friend, Mr. Adams, will want to know." She touched his cheek which fairly bristled in the morning sun. "With money I can skim off the top, you can print Mr. Adam's editorials and broadsides, if Mr. Wagner will let you as he has in the past."

In a breaking voice, Tyler said, "If you could only wait two years!"

He drew her close, closer than he had ever done before, and kissed her more deeply than he had ever done before, until his passion threatened to overcome them both. "Refuse to marry Blake, Meg! Just tell your father that you intend to marry me when I'm free in two years."

"You know I can't." She and Tyler had covered this ground before. "He'd most probably refuse to sign over the business to me, if I married you. He'd merge with Blake now and be done with it. Or just give up and die."

There was nothing wrong with Tyler Moore, except that he would never be rich. Neither Papa nor Mama would consider marriage to a poor man for their daughter, their only child. Once Robert asked permission to court her, they had thought of nothing else. The Blakes had status, after all! It was her duty to marry Robert! To make up for Mama's loss of so many children! To give Papa the assurance that Roberge Imports would continue, despite having no male heir! She was their only child, and only she could bring their dreams to fruition.

"Give it up for my sake, my darling Meg. Give it up, and be poor with me."

Give up her lifelong dream of independence?

Hating herself, she backed away. "You know I'd like nothing better," she told him, trying not to cry. "But I've been trained to run Roberge Imports, and I've dreamed of independence for years. And now that Papa has agreed, I can avoid coverture altogether."

Coverture was the legal term for the giving over of all assets a woman had to her new husband upon marriage.

"If Robert Blake agrees to it."

"Yes."

"Well? Does he?"

"He doesn't even know about it. But Papa is going to offer him a percentage of the profits as an inducement."

Tyler released her abruptly. "Your father must want this marriage quite a lot, to auction you off to the highest bidder."

The heat of anger flashed through her. She folded her hands tightly at her bodice, containing it. "That's a rotten thing to say, Tyler."

He drew a deep breath. "Will you accept my apology? T'was anger speaking."

"I know, I know." He was breaking her heart.

"We will always be friends, won't we?" The sadness in his eyes wrenched her.

"Always," she whispered. And did not add: one day maybe more than friends, if I have anything to say about it.

He kissed her hand in a sort of farewell, opened the storeroom door. "We'd better get back to the front, before Mr. Wagoner discovers I've closed the shop." Resigned, he hustled her out, unlocked the front door, put the sign away and set himself to appraising the advertisement. "That will be five pounds six. For running it in this week's Colonial Press and printing 8 posters. Agreeable?"

"Perfectly."

He set to writing up the invoice and a copy while she watched with an aching heart. As though the conversation in the back room were on-going, he said, "I don't think Mr. Adams will be writing editorials for a while. No one cares if parliament takes away their rights if they're preoccupied with defending themselves against a common enemy."

"What are you talking about?"

"Another war, of course. Parliament is taking charge of the French problem." Carefully he dripped the wax, when waited for the right moment to impress Wagner's seal upon it. "They've sent a general named Braddock and some of His Majesty's troops to Virginia, and they'll raise the local militia to reinforce the soldiers and go to the forks of the Ohio River and capture a French fort that's out there. Pretty soon our militia will be called—just wait and see—to capture others, just like before. The French will bring in troops from overseas or even their fleet—well, there's not much Adams can say with a war hanging over our heads."

Enoch Wagner, returning from his errands, stomped through the door. "I heard you closed us down, Mr. Tyler Moore, while I was out. Is that true?"

"Not exactly, sir. Miss Roberge came in to see if we could print this, sir." He held up the sketch of the Roberge advertisement.

"As soon as possible, Mr. Wagner," Margaret added.

"And so you shut up shop in order to discuss it, hey?" With a sardonic smile, he drew out his spectacles, examined the advertisement and then the bill Tyler had drawn up.

"Good! Well done, Mr. Moore. Hop to it, sir! The lady says they're in a hurry."

He waved a hand in the direction of the press, the issue of the shop closure forgotten—or deliberately overlooked. Tyler was as a son to him. Perhaps he would hire the boy, once his indenture was done.

And Margaret Roberge Blake would subsidize the printing of Samuel Adams' editorials, once the fervor of war was done, and meet the former bound boy in secret places, and do secret things. And if a child was the result, not even she would know whose it was. Tyler, like Robert, was Anglo-Saxon, blue-eyed, light-haired, fair of complexion.

With that in mind, the future looked much brighter.

CHAPTER

2

The Storm

The good ship *Lady Nan* wallowed, slipping down the side of one swell, lifting massively up the next. The guts of every passenger rose and sank with her, and the sky sulked, dull and dirty.

"I've heard of *mal de mer*," Mama gasped, hanging over the rail. "But I never knew how awful it was!" She retched again and yet again, and Margaret tried not to hear, tried not to think. Tried only to keep herself from retching too, her body stiff and sore and aching from endless hours of heaving and gagging.

How long had they been pitching and swaying out here in the endless gray ocean? They'd sailed out of Boston grandly, waving to Papa and Lucy and Cook and the Blakes, flags snapping and the sea splashing high along the bow. For several days they'd flown like a bird, dipping down one wave, up the next, which was the beginning of their misery. Then they'd been becalmed for a time, during which the constant nausea settled back and allowed them to eat a bit, and sleep, and regain their strength.

Now, after a three day respite, the ocean had again become troubled and although there was no wind, the swells had grown and the waves had arisen, pitching *Lady Nan* up and then down, up and then down, and the seasickness returned.

"I haven't seen the captain for a while," Mr. Thomas Randall of Milton grumbled, perched on the anchor chain. "I'll wager he's swilling rum in his cabin. No doubt he's been drunk the whole time."

"Or else he's seasick himself," Margaret offered.

"Huh!" he snorted, offended that this mere slip of a girl would contradict him. Yet it was true that some mariners took a while to recover their sea-legs, no matter how experienced they were.

A breath of air stirred the listless sails, then fell away.

"Did you feel that?" Mama whispered in Margaret's ear.

"Feel what?"

"A breeze. A bit of a breeze."

One of the enormous sails above them flapped against its web of ratlines and stays. The bored crew instantly looked up. The sails flapped again and an order was bawled out, sounding small in the ocean vastness. The men began to run, scattering throughout the ship. Some climbed the rigging, some stowed gear, others fetched hammers and started nailing the hatches and portholes shut.

"Hey!" Mr. Randall called to a sailor scampering by. "You! Young fellow! What's happening?"

"Storm approaching, sir," the sailor called back over his shoulder.

"Sometimes it happens after a long stretch of dead weather, sir," said another, hurrying behind the first. "You'll have to go below."

"Oh, my, let's not," Mama moaned. Margaret fought the nausea that rose at the very idea of descending into that vile hole, made putrid by seasick passengers. She decided not to think about it. Tried to put it in the little corner of her mind along with the other thoughts that she and Mama had agreed not to dwell upon—like weevils in the biscuits, cider with mold floating on its surface, water that smelled of the slimy wooden cask in which it was stored. They had also agreed to put out of their minds the possibility of getting lost, or besieged by a whale, or being overtaken by pirates. But if any pirates were nearby, they had been becalmed too, and were also waiting for the wind to rise before venturing to capture anything. And now—lo and behold—the wind was rising. Was there a ship—any ship—on the horizon? Pirate or otherwise?

Margaret looked carefully, but the endless Atlantic was clear, while the mounting breeze plucked at the edges of her cloak and fingered the hood that covered her hair. The ship's sails slowly filled and the *Lady Nan* began to run with purpose through the sea. The metal-colored sky held black clouds now, with lightning leaping from one to the other. The sea splintered and grew confused and the horizon became smudged and vague.

"Down you go! Look lively now!"

The passengers were herded to the ladder and urged—then pushed—below deck. Dreading it, Margaret followed Mama down, kicking her petticoats out of the way while she felt for each rung. When everyone was at the bottom, they huddled together and watched as the hatch cover was pulled into place overhead and nailed tight. Slowly they moved through the dim, nasty, stinking corridor as though in a funeral procession, making their way to their respective cabins. Two oil lamps were suspended from the overhead beams, winking and fluttering; unsatisfactory as they were for light, their low glow was comforting. After she was sure Mama was settled in her bunk, Margaret moved a trunk into the entrance of their little cabin, ensuring lantern light. The door would not swing shut, sealing them into darkness—not if she could help it!

It was narrow, the cabin, with just enough room for one person to stand. Airless, without windows or amenities of any kind, Margaret loathed it as she would loathe a coffin.

"Don't climb up to your bunk yet, darling. Stay here with me." Mama moved as far over as she could. "We can hold on to each other."

"Gladly!" Margaret exclaimed, grateful for the suggestion. Removing one of her petticoats and rolling it up into a pillow, she tucked herself in and spooned with Mama, who threw a protective arm around her.

"I think we'd better pray, don't you?"

"Yes, Mama. You start."

The ship lurched; Mama's hold tightened. "Lord, protect us in this, our hour of need," she prayed into Margaret's ear. "If we have done badly, forgive us. If we have not done what we should have done, forgive us."

Belatedly, Margaret thought about Tyler. Had her dalliance with him, in defiance of her father, angered the Deity? Or her schemes for a later day, once she was married and Tyler was no longer indentured?

Please, God, she petitioned the Unknown, please forgive me this trespass.

"Protect us, Lord," she said, loud enough for Mama to hear. "I'm sorry I don't pray more. I will, if I have the chance, I promise! Keep Father and Lucy safe and well."

"And Aunt Rose and Uncle Alexander and Cousin Montague . . ." Mama came from a large family who lived in Virginia and seemed to have produced dozens of children, all of whom, miraculously, lived. Margaret listened with half an ear.

The wind rose and rose and cried in anguished melancholy. Only a few inches away, on the other side of the planking, the angry Atlantic pounded, seeking a way to get inside the ship.

Mon dieu, pourquois nous as-tu abandonne? My God, why have you abandoned us? Perhaps the Almighty would hear better if they prayed in French.

CHAPTER TWO

Above the roar of the wind and sea something shattered. A spar perhaps—though how could anyone know, locked below as they were? Locked up tight, without any way to escape....

She and Mama clung to one another, beyond speech or even tears, while the other passengers moaned and cried and prayed loudly, and endless time crawled by, on and on as the ship battled the sea.

We are not going to sink, she insisted. Many a ship—most ships—survive a storm. That's why they batten down the hatches. To keep the craft floating like a corked bottle. The air is trapped inside. Like we, ourselves, are trapped, she observed unwillingly.

One of the lamps in the corridor went out, drowned in its own oil; the one remaining went low, fluttered up again. The wind beyond the confines of their corked bottle rose to an even higher pitch, and the ship drove on, on.

She must keep her mind occupied. If she busied herself thinking, the time would go by faster. Tyler Moore was the most important person in her life, aside from her family. Thinking about their meeting in the back room of Wagner's shop, thinking about him and everything he'd been through would fill her thoughts, most certainly. He had begun life as the son of a successful businessman, who, with his mercantile associates, had formed a landbank. Among his associates was Deacon Adams, father of Samuel whom Tyler so much admired. The Landbank proprietors printed their own money, accepting land as security for a loan—fields, woodlots, bogs, and for a year everything had worked perfectly, until parliament judged the whole scheme illegal, citing an obscure paragraph in the colony's charter. Not only was the bank shut down, but the proprietors were held liable, and were required to redeem the mortgages—in cash.

Of course, no one had cash. One by one the proprietors went bankrupt, sold their houses and their family jewelry and dress clothing and went back to work as the tradesmen they once had been. Samuel Adams father, a maltster, returned to brewing beer. Tyler's father sold his business and found work in a counting house—a position far beneath his capabilities. Then his eldest son, Tyler's brother, had died at Louisbourg. The family homestead was sold to satisfy the Landbank loans. When Tyler was fifteen years old, he was apprenticed to Enoch Wagner, who could provide for him better than his own father could. Soon after, Mr. Moore became ill—very ill—and died. The younger children were placed in homes of relatives . . . .

A long, sharp scraping ran the length of the hull, like a gigantic fingernail across a huge slate. The ship was wrenched violently and a ripping, a rendering began slowly, slowly, and then the ship slammed into something enormously hard, enormously unyielding. It stopped and tipped. The passengers were thrown from their bunks. Margaret and Mama struggled together on the floor of the cabin while the *Lady Nan* lifted, her timbers shuddering and cracking. Icy air swept through the hold, the thunder of surf growled nearby. In screeching, howling agony, *Lady Nan* was rendered in twain, mortally wounded and dying fast.

A wall of water rushed through the doorway and up the walls of the cabin. Horrified, Margaret was torn from Mama's arms, sucked into the sea where the jaws of a freezing hell opened wide, pulling her down and down. In the blackness that surrounded her, the waves echoed distantly until the beating of her heart grew louder and louder and her chest began to burn. And then she was hurled to the surface, a piece of flotsam among other pieces.

Gasping, she flailed and kicked, determined not to sink again. Nearby, very, very near, was the crash of surf. A wave lifted her high, cast her down and back up; distantly the passengers cried, their voices kitten-like above the cacophony.

CHAPTER TWO

Suddenly she heard the cursing of men nearly on top of her.
"*Merde!*" Shit!
"*Bon sang!*" Damn it!
A small wooden boat bounced up on the crest of a wave, then was lost to sight in a trough.
"*Quelqu'un est là! Regardez!*" Someone is there. Look!
Their voices were small in the roaring of the storm.
"Help!" she screamed. "Help me! Oh, please . . ."
The little boat reappeared, and over its side a bearded face stared down. Her wrists were caught just as a wave reached for her; strong arms pried her from its grasp, lifted her up and dropped her onto the bottom of a dory. Then there was counting.
Un.
Deux.
Trois.
Un.
Deux . . . .
Showered with salt spray, cold and miserable beyond anything she had ever experienced, Margaret curled up tightly into a ball.
The little boat pulled free of the surf as the four men at the oars strained and panted and called to every saint.
"*Elle tremble,*" observed one of the oarsmen. She shivers. "She will die of exposure!"
"*Merde,*" panted another, ripping off his coat and throwing it over her, then instantly returning to the beat.
She huddled under it as the dory plunged through the howling gale and ugly sea until, without warning, the broad side of a ship hulked high above them. A rope ladder was tossed down; one of the oarsmen, balancing her on his shoulder, carried her up and up and onto the deck.

The ship's pitching was mild compared to that of the dingy.

"*Le navire Anglais s'est brisé.* The English brig breaks apart," one of the men shouted above the wind. "We heard the cries of other passengers, but only the girl could we take from the water before we, too, would be smashed."

"This waif, then, is a girl?"

"*Oui, mon capitaine.*"

"Well, don't just stand here. Take her to my quarters where she will be sheltered."

Broad shoulders protected her as she was carried up to the quarterdeck and into the cabin.

"Think you this girl is *Anglais?*" asked someone. Someone male.

"*Elle doit être.* She must be. The passengers—the ones we could not reach, were calling to *le bon Dieu* in English."

"She called to us in English, too."

"Her garment is wet," someone observed. "It should be removed."

"We shall be of assistance," volunteered others, and before the implications became apparent, her dress was torn off, and her chemise and stays as well.

"*Elle est bleu partout.* She is blue all over," they exclaimed.

"Good Christ, have you no mercy?" One of them wrapped a blanket around her, bundled her onto a built-in bed. "Find more covers," he said. "Many of them. Dry, if possible. Quickly."

She lay entombed under the blanket until the cabin door was flung open again, and the wind rushed in along with more men who forced the door shut.

"*Couvertures.* Blankets," one said, and more were piled on.

"Does the captain wish to interview her?"

"*Oui.* He comes now."

The screeching wind announced his entrance.

"So this *donc ce morceau*, this lump, it is a girl?" the voice of the captain asked.

"*Oui.*"

"Have you learned if the ship was out of Boston or out of *Londres?*"

"*Nous ne savons pas.* We know not."

"You asked *la jeune fille?* The girl?"

"No, sir. We just hoped she would not die. Regard her, how she just lies there. *La pauvre!* The poor thing!"

"She speaks not?"

"No sir. Not yet."

"Young? Old?"

"Young. Very young. The tits, they are upright. *Son cul est ferme.* The ass, it is firm."

"And round, like a melon," added another. "Virgin more than likely."

Beneath her blankets, Margaret became hot, aware, finally, that they were describing her naked body.

"Very well. LeBlanc will speak with her when this *tempete monstrueuse arrete*, when this fucking storm stops. He knows English. Meanwhile, she is fine where she is. We have a ship to sail. *Allons-nous!*"

They shuffled away, leaving her naked and curled up like a snail inside a shell of scratchy wool. The warmth of her humiliation embraced her, carrying her out onto the tide of sleep where she drifted dreamless until the nightmare began, a nightmare of a wild, sucking sea, of the pitching cabin in the hold of *Lady Nan*, of Mama's mouth—a black hole of a mouth—screaming without sound, and then filling up with sand . . . .

"*Mademoiselle!*" A man's voice.

Within the blankets all was dark.

"*Mademoiselle!*" The man opened a small gap at the edge of her coverings, sending gusts of coldness over her. "Speak, *Mademoiselle!*"

She must say something lest he uncover her completely. Unwillingly, she reached through the gap.

"Ah! *Te voila!* There you are!"

Crouching down to speak into the hole was a small man in wet clothes that dripped on the floor. "*Bienvenue, Mademoiselle!* Welcome! I am Pierre LeBlanc, and I speak the English, as you see."

"'Lo," she moaned.

"*Regarde!* Look!" He turned away. "She wakes!"

"Proceed, *s'il vous plait*," ordered a familiar voice. "Please."

"*Oui. Mademoiselle!* We have brought you a mug of hot tea. Will you sit up and partake of it?"

Tea! Oh, tea! She struggled into an upright position, hurting in every muscle and bone and through the opening in the cave, took the hot cup. The tea's aroma was wondrous; its heat radiated into every crevice of her brain and body and she closed her eyes, letting it comfort her.

"I wish to ask you about your ship," the man leBlanc persisted, turning the edge of the blanket back further so that he could see her face. "Can you understand my English?" Over his shoulder, he said to the captain, "*J'ai pas eu beaucoup de pratique ces dernier temps*. I have not had much practice of late."

"It is better than nothing, *certainement*," the authoritative voice said.

Nearly telling the man LeBlanc—in French—that his English was fine, Margaret came awake enough to realize that since all of them were obviously French, they might be the enemy. Hastily checking to make sure she was sufficiently covered, she swallowed the tea as fast as she could, hoping to bring her wits back, and accommodated LeBlanc by facing him.

"Thank you, sir, for the tea!" She spoke slowly, enunciating clearly.

"Are you feeling well enough now to talk?" LeBlanc asked. "Can you tell us the name of your ship?"

"*Lady Nan.*" Her voice cracked.

"*Pardone moi?*" The man cupped his ear.

"*Lady Nan.*"

The ship was called *Madame Nan*," LeBlanc said to the captain. Turning back to her, he asked, "From whence sailed *Madame Nan?*"

With an effort she focused on the question. "Boston."

"*Quand at-elle quitte?* When did she leave?"

She thought about it, about the morning so long ago when everyone was waving and blowing kisses and the wharves of Boston became smaller and smaller. "May fifth."

"*Cinq mai,*" Le Blanc told the captain. "Where bound?"

"London."

"You were not on course." LeBlank's accent was thick, and just in time she stopped herself from asking him, in French, to repeat the question. "*Madame Nan* was very far northeast of Boston. Far from the usual shipping lanes. Why was that?"

"The wind died down. We floated around a long time. Then the storm overtook us."

"It was a big storm," he agreed pleasantly. "But nearly over now. Fear not." The wind was no longer howling, she realized.

"Has anyone been found from the *Lady Nan*, besides me?"

"Lamentably, I regret to announce—no."

Mama, then, was gone. Irretrievably gone. And all those other poor passengers below deck. Her eyes filled.

"I have just informed her that there were no other survivors," LeBlanc told the captain in French. The two men crossed themselves, an alien gesture.

"Where are we now?" she asked in an effort to keep her mind away from the lost souls aboard *Lady Nan*, and the soul of Mama.

Mama!

"We approach Louisbourg, on *Île Royale*."

Louisbourg! Where Tyler Moore's brother died!

"We will anchor in the harbor there, and discover what we are to do about you." The man LeBlanc went on, enunciating clearly, speaking slowly for her benefit. "Our ship is called *L'Esperance de Dieu*. Hope of God. We are of Quebec City, but we work under the Louisbourg commandant. When the ice of winter disperses, we venture out. We seek the English shipping lanes. You were blown into our path."

It seemed clear that stupidity would serve her better than anything else. "For what reason do you seek them?" she asked childishly.

"We relieve them of their cargoes!" He laughed jovially, as though this were the world's greatest joke. "The lanes of the ships between England and *Amerique*—we cross them, we wait for the ships, they fall into our net. Understand you?"

"So you are pirates."

"Please, *Mademoiselle*!" he protested. "Pirates are no better than thieves. We sail under a Lettre of Marque—in service to the Fleur de Lys—by order of King Louis!"

"I believe Letters of Marque are only issued in time of war," she observed. "Have hostilities begun?"

LeBlanc shrugged. He looked over his shoulder again and up at the captain. "She is not stupid, this little girl," he said, and returned to the task at hand. "You sailed from Boston, then, on the fifth of May."

"Yes."

"You travelled with *votre maman*? Your mother?"

Her sudden tears told them the answer.

"She knows nothing," LeBlanc said to the captain. "Can we not let her alone now? Doubtless she needs privacy. She is in mourning. Her mother sailed also on *Madam Nan*."

"Ah," sighed the other, and again the men crossed themselves.

"We shall try to find clothing she can wear. Inform her of this," the captain ordered.

"Very well." LeBlanc turned back to her. "Now, *Mademoiselle*—" he paused. "What is your name?"

It would be an added complication, would it not, to give them a name so obviously French as Roberge?

She rallied. "Robinson," she said. "Margaret Robinson." Indeed, a very English name!

"*Alors*, Miss Robinson. You will be unharmed. You need worry not."

"Please, sir," she begged, and her tears threatened to return. "I just want to go home."

LeBlanc turned to the captain. "She wishes to return to Boston," he said in French. "Shall I assure her that we will arrange for this for her?"

"*Non!*" the captain growled. "No. If she is lonely and frightened, she will be more obedient. We will drop her off at Louisbourg. It will be up to the Commandant to decide what to do. He'll either take her to Halifax and let the British transport her to Boston, or else use her for a prisoner exchange if there's need for one."

Prisoner exchange? To hide what must be an expression of dismay, she turned away, rolling up in her blankets once again.

"Tell her she is to stay here. She is not to leave. She is not to go on deck. I do not want her distracting the men—and there's not a woman alive who would not flaunt herself under these circumstances."

"The captain says you may stay here, *Mademoiselle*," LeBlanc told her blanketed self, diplomatically abbreviating the message.

"Tell him thank you," she responded, her voice muffled by the covers.

"She says thank you," LeBlanc reported.

"Tell her it is nothing," the captain growled, and stomped out of the cabin.

"He says you're welcome," LeBlanc repeated dutifully. "You will need something to wear. I shall search for a small jacket and pants. Unfortunately, we do not carry dresses." He chuckled at his own humor. His footsteps became distant, then disappeared as the door was secured from the outside, eliminating the possibility of her wandering about the quarterdeck.

So she could be exchanged, like an article of trade! She did not like that, not at all. Surely it would be better to go to Halifax. It was in Nova Scotia, and Nova Scotia was controlled by the British, her own people. She would be safe there.

Yet they seemed not to want to harm her, these French thugs. For this she was grateful. The thugs seemed quite certain that she would get home again—one way or another. And if it was decided she must travel someplace, somewhere in the hinterland of New France, to be exchanged, perhaps they would transport her in a sedan chair, and think to put curtains on it. If there were insects flying about, a curtain would help a little, besides giving her privacy.

Unbidden, her tears rose again. It did not matter that tomorrow she would see for herself the famous military installation—Louisbourg—the fort that had held New England by the throat for years. That had taken the life of Tyler's brother and then had been returned so the enemy was free to continue ravaging American ships. All she could do, about any of it, was cry, and this she did until her eyes, despite anything she might do, fell shut and she lay down again and slept.

CHAPTER

3

Louisbourg

Out from the silence and mystery of fog, Louisbourg emerged. A low lying mist hovered over the sheltered harbor and swirled about the King's bastion. Its disembodied clock tower watched over the countless vessels that were scattered across the crowded cove. *L'Esperance de Dieu* worked her way into their midst and dropped anchor, her chain rattling monstrously in the shrouded quiet.

The cabin had been unlocked, and Margaret watched from its doorway as a dory was lowered. An oarsman followed it down the rope ladder, and then the captain with the ship's log. They were swallowed up, only the soft strokes of the oars notifying the world that they were present somewhere in the fog.

Then a quick upspringing breeze cleared some of the mist away, and she had a glimpse of the Bourbon royal coat of arms over the bastion gate. As quickly, the fog returned and she shivered despite her heavy clothes: a knitted cap that kept her hair hidden, a long woolen tunic beneath a large coat that fell to her knees, and low-cut boots, several sizes larger than her feet.

Another teasing glimpse of the shoreline showed dark wooden shanties huddled above the high tide mark, their chimneys smoking in profusion, adding cloud-like layers to the fog. From an unseen source a procession of carts was winding single file toward the fortress and the city within its walls.

LeBlanc appeared. "Louisbourg uses 350 cords of wood a year." He waved at the carts. "The fortress has need of fuel all summer—and in the winter too, of course."

"There is forest somewhere near, then?" The brief glance she'd had showed a landscape stripped of trees.

"There is much forest. Inland. More even than you can imagine."

"And those peasants bring fuel to town? Do they get paid?"

"The Acadians," he said emphatically. "It is great rudeness to call them peasants. And yes, they receive remuneration."

"Acadians?"

"The original settlers of what you English believe is Nova Scotia. Their country is Acadia, no matter what the English say. It will always be Acadia."

He was becoming red-faced. British control of Nova Scotia, established by treaty forty years ago in yet another war with France, was apparently still a sore subject.

Becoming visible through the thinning fog was an enormous dock running parallel to the water. Set back from it were shops and warehouses. In the center a cobbled thoroughfare sloped gently up, lined with dwellings, one immediately next to the other. Thick stone walls surrounded the entire city, and a single gate, near the waterfront, gave access to the countryside.

"Does everyone live inside the walls?" she asked.

"The French do, yes. They are the shopkeepers and bakers and families of the officers."

"I saw some huts beyond the city walls. Who lives in them?"

"It is that many Acadians are fleeing here, to *Île Royale*, and also *Île St. Jean*, which is nearby. Both belong to France. There is trouble, you see, about the oath."

"What oath?"

He sighed, summoning patience with her questions. "The English wish the Acadians to take an oath of allegiance to your King."

"Well," she observed, "that seems reasonable, since Nova Scotia is his. And has been, for quite a while."

"Acadians are French Catholics, *Mademoiselle*. There is a priest who leads them, and tells them to resist. This they are happy to do. But now the English threaten to deport them if they will not sign, so they come to *Île Royale* and, as I said, also *Île St. Jean*. They cannot be deported from French territory."

There was a hail from below; the dory had returned.

Up over the rail rose the captain and his logbook. "LeBlanc," he shouted. "Where the fuck are you?!"

"*Voici*—here!" LeBlanc shouted back. He did not appear embarrassed by the crudity of the captain. But, of course, he assumed Margaret did not understand it. Hopefully her face had not turned red. Quickly she coughed, hard enough and long enough to cause pinkness in any case.

"I hope you are not getting *pneumonie!*" LeBlanc exclaimed.

She waved away his concern.

"Load the girl into the dory and take her to Carrerot," the captain ordered. "She must be ready to depart late this afternoon."

"*Ou-va-t-elle?* Where goes she?"

"Fort Lawrence. The English are holding a prisoner there. Father LeLoutre wants him back."

"So she will be exchanged, no?"

"*Exactement.* Is she ready to leave *L'Esperance de Dieu?*"

"She is." Turning to her, Le Blanc urged, "Come with me." Holding out his hand, he led her to the rail, secured his footing on the ladder, and gestured for her to scramble over the edge. Using the rung just above his so that he could steady her, they scrabbled their way down and stepped into the little boat, nearly capsizing it.

Fort Lawrence. She had never heard of it, but could ask nothing without betraying her knowledge of French. "Am I to remain here, in the city?" she asked instead, allowing LeBlanc to seat her in the stern.

"For a while, yes. You shall rest yourself at the home of Andre Carrerot. He speaks no English, but you are not to worry. We shall arrange everything, Carrerot and I, to help you get back to Boston when the opportunity presents itself."

"Is this Andre Carrerot your leader?"

"A liaison. Between the Acadians and the Mi'kmaqs and the French." The oarsman pulled them quickly across the harbor.

"What is a Mi'kmaq?"

He took a deep breath, again summoning patience with her endless questions. "The kind of Indian that lives in these parts. They have always lived here, longer than anyone can remember."

"Are they dangerous?"

"They can be, if aroused. The English are building forts now, and have not asked their permission. I believe they are very angry."

"Why should they be asked for permission?"

"The land is theirs, *Mademoiselle*. They must be consulted before any building is erected. The British have offended them, and the soldiers do well to avoid them."

"Dare I ask why?"

"And I—dare I ask if you have heard of ritual torture?"

Rather wishing she had kept her mouth shut, she shook her head.

"On the prisoner of war—a male prisoner—they commit acts that will bring him great pain, prolonged pain. I would rather not tell you more, *Mademoiselle*."

"And I do not wish to hear more!"

"You are not to worry. They do not usually torture women. They take them into the tribe, and eventually sell them or marry them."

And this was supposed to make her feel better?

"The Acadians—they get on well with the natives?"

"They do. You see, they are farmers, and use the land carefully and well, do not hunt or wander around in Mi'kmaq domains. They have lived together happily for many years."

The dory sidled up to a set of steps built into the wharf, and offering his arm so that she might use them without getting her feet wet, LeBlanc helped her to pass under the city's arched gate. Sentries, stern and incurious in buff colored coats with blue facings, guarded it, pikes at the ready.

A wooden walkway ran the length of the quay, giving access to smithys, markets, gun shops, cobblers, clothing, barbers. Carts streamed by, full of furs and firewood. Casks were piled high everywhere. Merchants and soldiers mixed and mingled. Some civilians were out and about their business now that the fog had lifted—tradesmen with their rough, drab clothes, lowly women shopping, bags of goods hanging at their sides, boys running errands for the gentry, as yet unseen, and herself—scuffling along in boots so large she nearly stepped out of them. LeBlanc took her arm as they turned onto the central cobbled street that climbed up the gradual rise to the back wall of the city.

"Carrerot lives up here. I am quite sure he will not be at home when we arrive, but you will be made welcome." He guided her around refuse and offal and pedestrians. "He arranges foodstuffs and armaments and uniforms that supply the garrison. On his own ships."

As a business woman herself, Margaret saw that Carrerot was a very shrewd man, in control of imports and exports and their means of coming in and going out.

Fog appeared again, along with a fine drizzle. She pulled her huge wool coat closer and her knitted cap lower; LeBlanc put a protective arm around her and they struggled on, stopping at a recessed doorway. He knocked.

A housemaid, demure in a boring brown dress and an apron well covered with flour opened the door. "Ah! Monsieur LeBlanc! *Bonjour!*" She smiled at both of them. "*Entrez, s'il vous plait!* Come in! I will fetch Madame."

They dripped onto a stone floor and waited at the foot of a broad and gracious stairway. The receiving rooms, apparently, were on the second floor, just as they were in Boston's finer homes. Not in hers, for the Roberge family was not rich enough for that. Yet.

Home. She must not think about home, lest tears begin.

A stout woman covered chin to toe with a large, flour-dusted smock came toward them from the back of the house, wiping her hands and holding out embracing arms. "Leblanc!" She kissed his cheeks, as he did hers, both of them careful not to leave traces of flour on his clothes. "*Une plaisir*, a pleasure, to see you. And this is the prisoner?"

"The guest," reproved LeBlanc. "*Une jeune fille.*" A girl. He lifted the knitted hat, and Margaret's hair fell abundantly down her back.

The woman nodded. "Ah. So I see. We heard only that there was one, but we did not hear about its gender."

"And here she is. We picked her out of the sea."

"Has she not a garment appropriate?"

"Unfortunately, she has none at all. This is the best we could give her, since we do not carry female clothing, as a rule." They chuckled together over this ludicrous idea.

I had a dress once, she wanted to say, but I don't know what they did with it.

"Where is Carrerot?" asked LeBlanc.

"At the garrison. He told me only that the prisoner must be ready by late afternoon. Duval will take her to Fort Lawrence where there is a man the French wish to liberate."

Le Blanc turned to Margaret who waited with an expressionless face that gave no hint of her ability to understand everything they had said. "Madame Carrerot bids you welcome," he simpered. Which, of course, was not true.

"Pray thank her."

LeBlanc turned to the woman. "If she is going to travel with Duval, she'll need boys clothing. He cannot take a girl into the wilderness. About the size of an eleven year *garçon*, no?"

"*Oui*," agreed Madam Carrorot, sizing up her guest. "And she'll need a pack of her own, with such things as a female might require. Assuming she is old enough."

LeBlanc reddened. "I know not," he said. "And I hope you understand that I will not inquire, Jeanne."

"Has she tits?" Madam Carrerot indicated her own massive bosom.

"*Oui*. Very pretty ones."

Jeanne Carrerot nodded wisely. "I shall see to it, then. If you would be so kind as to explain to her that she will meet Duval later, that we will bring dinner to her before then, and that we will provide a new set of clothing? MARIE!" she roared.

The maid appeared from the kitchen. "Yes, Madame?"

"Take water and blankets to the attic. Then bring one of your shifts to me."

Like a wraith, the girl disappeared.

"Is it necessary? The lock?" asked LeBlanc.

The two of them looked over the disheveled creature in their midst. "If she escaped, Carrerot would be very displeased," Madame pointed out. "Not to mention Father LaLoutre. And Bonsoleil, the Acadian leader. Paul-Henri is important to them."

Paul-Henri. Ah! The mysterious man had a name!

"Where in the name of *le bon Dieu* would she go, if she were to escape? The young lady is *Bostonnais*, and wishes to return home. Hardly can she walk there! She has nothing to gain in trying to escape."

"Does she understand this? Does she know she likely will be exchanged?"

"Perhaps not," the man admitted. "I was told to reveal as little as possible to her."

"Exchange is more than Paul-Henri deserves! That man, I detest him! Duval is rough enough, but Paul-Henri is an animal."

"Still, he is a fighter formidable," pointed out LeBlanc. "So we must hope that the commander *americain* will consider this girl important enough to exchange for him."

Important enough! Margaret remembered to look away before indignation showed on her face. As though she had nothing else in mind but its adornments, she examined the entry hall, its portraits, its shield, its coat of arms.

"Your transport is being arranged," LeBlanc told her. "Meanwhile, there is a pleasant, private room in the attic," he continued smoothly. "You will be safe there, until arrangements can be made, and Mme Carrerot will see that you have a warm meal, and later on Monsieur Carrerot will arrange your transport."

"Tell her she will have clothes to wear," said Madam Carrerot, turning to the back of the house. "MARIE!" she roared again.

"Here I am," the girl called, hurrying to the entry. "I have found her a shift." She held it out for Madam's inspection.

But Madam did not so much as glance at it. "*Bien.* Good. Take the girl to the attic. Then come back and help me with the bread. Go!" She made shoo-ing motions to both girls.

"Follow the maid. I will see you later," LeBlanc reassured her. "Rest well."

What else could she do? The maid Marie led her to the back of the house and up a narrow flight of stairs, and then another where there was a tiny room beneath the eaves with a streak of sun slashing the floor.

The girl gave her the shift, ducked a small curtsey and propelled her inside with a gentle push, drew the door shut and locked it.

Again she was a prisoner, in as small a space as she'd had on the ship in the galley. The sunstreak on the floor faded, then brightened again. She went to the window. Below was a large courtyard, surrounded by the backsides of many houses and crisscrossed with flagstoned paths that wound around gardens in raised beds. A privy with the branches of a fruit tree tied in orderly tiers against its sunny side stood nearby the communal well in the center, and she saw a woman come out to fill a bucket and return to wherever she belonged. A door far below faintly banged shut.

It would be good to get out of her damp garments. Shrugging off the heavy coat, pulling off the hat and tunic, kicking the boots away, she slipped the shift over her head, relieved to feel the smooth caress of linen against her skin. The rough wool tunic had chaffed; the shift was a welcomed change. Now more comfortable, she looked around the room. There was a narrow cot tucked under the eaves, with several folded blankets on it, a chair and small commode by the door.

The sunlight on the floor moved quickly as she lay down, pulled the blankets around her and thought about the man Duval who would probably take her to Fort Lawrence. Wherever that might be. Who was Duval? A rough man. Was that not what Mme. Carrerot had said? But not as bad as the other one, whom they wanted in exchange.

The sun disappeared, and within a moment a steady rain tapped on the window, as though to tell her she was not as alone as she felt. Beneath the blankets heat was starting to accumulate, and her body slowly dissolved into that soft center of herself. Staring at the slanted ceiling so close to her face, she felt sleep creeping up on her again and gratefully let it take her away, blotting out the long empty hours of waiting, while the sun and clouds and fog chased each other across the face of the day.

CHAPTER
4

Duval

Footsteps on the stairs. A key rasping in the lock.
"*Mademoiselle*! I enter!" LeBlanc opened the door, awkwardly stood on the threshold, carrying a pile of clothing and a pack.

"You ate not your dinner!" he exclaimed. "The maid Marie was worried when she saw the dishes right where she left them, untouched."

Margaret yawned, sat up, gestured for him to enter and set the clothes beside her—a short-gown to wear beneath a rough-spun linen tunic that fell to her knees, long woolen tubes with ties at one end.

"Leggins," he explained. "You attach them as you would your skirts and apron."

High soft leather boots, into which to tuck the leggins. A boy's cap, which, unlike the knitted one she'd been wearing, was too small to hold her hair, and a knee length quilted jacket. "It will be cold on the ocean," LeBlanc explained. "You will need it then."

"The ocean! I am going back to Boston, Monsieur LeBlanc?"

"In a manner of speaking, *oui*. And we will have to cut your hair," LeBlanc went on. "Then the cap will fit."

"Surely, sir, that is not necessary!"

"You are to look like a boy. You cannot have such long hair."

"I will tuck it under the knitted hat I wore this morning."

"And it might come off, and your hair would fall down your back, as it does now. It must go." He ducked and fetched a jug he'd left by the door. "Here is water with which to refresh yourself." From his pockets he dredged up a hunk of cheese, a heel of bread.

"Is the water safe to drink?" Boston water—the water in any city, she supposed—was unclean. Pouring some into the cup, she tasted it and found it was like fresh air, cool and without flavor of any kind. Remarkable!

"The clothes, put on. The food, eat, and the water drink. Freshen yourself. Come downstairs when I call," LeBlanc instructed. "We expect Duval soon."

Then he was gone. Pouring out more water into the bowl on the commode, she washed as best she could, then pulled on the leggings, tying the strings around her waist. The tunic resisted the shortgown, but she finally was able to pull that on, too, smoothing both of them over the unfamiliar leggings. The boots came next, only a little too large, and the small, inadequate cap. She stuffed it into the jacket pocket and then waited, nibbling at the bread and cheese, sipping and savoring the water, thinking of home, strong now with knowing that sooner or later, she would be there once more . . . .

❧

The second floor receiving room was mellow in the early summer afternoon's light. The windows were framed with heavily embroidered drapery tied back with tassled cords; the chairs were veritable thrones with elegantly curved legs, and small, equally elegant occasional tables were scattered here and there. Woven wool carpeting decorated with delicate vines and flowers covered the wooden floor, and wall hangings depicting damsels in gardens kept any errant drafts out. It was a room decorated in high French style, glowing with a golden charm.

LeBlanc had led her to a chair next to Madame Carrerot, then stood behind it, waiting for the mysterious Marc Duval. Monsieur Carrerot took a throne across from them and smoked a pipe, his foot swinging in rhythm to a beat heard only by himself. Sitting on her hands to hide their shaking, Margaret clamped her knees tight, for without long skirts and petticoats, there was little to protect her modesty. Her leggings were tied separately around her waist and her tunic fell only to her knees. She saw Monsieur Carrerot glance at her now and again, as though hoping for a glimpse of something no girl ever showed to anyone. She crossed the ankles of her high boots, into which the leggings were tucked. On her head was the knitted hat, under which she'd stuffed her hair. The pack Madam Carrerot had put together for her lay beneath her chair, filled with an extra set of boy's clothing in case the ones she was wearing got impossibly soiled, a towel and sponge and wadding for her monthly time. On top of the bag was the quilted jacket with the too-small cap in its pocket.

Monsieur Carrerot spoke fluent English. "Miss Robinson, you understand that we are arranging for your transport back to Boston?"

"Yes, sir."

"We have a scout, named Marc Duval."

"Yes, I have heard the name."

"Duval is much respected by the Acadians and Mi'kmaqs. He is a man much trusted by Bonsoleil—Joseph Broussard—who leads the Acadians in war."

"War!"

"*Oui, Mademoiselle.* Acadia is at war with your king. The Mi'kmaqs have joined them in forcing out the English who have been brought here to settle. Bonsoleil takes his direction from Father LeLoutre, who has always resisted incursions of the Protestants. Thus we have three distinct forces that are allied against the British in this war: we, the French; the natives; and the Acadians."

He waved his hand dismissively. "Then, there are woodsmen who know the natives well and have traded with them for years. It is from this class that Marc Duval comes. Please be obedient to his requests and keep as silent as possible in his presence."

"Does this man, Duval, speak English?"

"He does."

The knocker on the street door was pounded with vigor; the maid's slippers whispered in the downstairs hall as she hurried to answer. There was muffled conversation; the girl raced up to the second floor.

"*Pardon, Madame et Monsieur*—here is a caller who says he will not wait to be announced . . ."

"Do not worry, Marie," *Monsieur* Carrerot assured her. "We are expecting him."

The girl hesitated. Dipping a courtesy of acquiescence, she backed away, but did not leave the room. Instead, her eyes were fastened on the stranger who now appeared, stair by stair; dark hair, tied back, clean shaven, tanned face and throat, a huntsman's tunic and a loose leather jerkin, leggings, moccasins with tattered beadwork on them. Taller than most Frenchmen, his face was strong-featured, with a firm mouth that seemed grim just now. He brought the smell of wood smoke in with him, and a feral scent.

Carrerot rose and bowed although his station was undoubtedly much higher than that of Duval. "Marc! *Un plaisir*, as always."

Duval nodded in acknowledgement, bowed to Carrerot's wife, nodded toward LeBlanc.

"You may leave, Marie," Carrerot instructed the maid, who reluctantly did so, taking one last peek at the visitor before descending the stairs. "Will you be seated?" he asked Duval.

"Thank you, no." He did not offer an excuse for his refusal, and Carrerot remained standing. They stared down at Margaret, demurely waiting.

"A girl," he observed, disgust in his tone.

"*Oui.* But looking like a boy, as you can see."

"Take off the cap," he requested in English, looking directly at her.

Oh, no, she thought as she complied and her hair, snarled and dirty, cascaded down.

"Why has her hair not been cut?"

His aggravation at this apparent oversight lowered the temperature in the room considerably. Madam Carrerot rose. "She seemed very resistant and we were not sure you would be willing to take her," she explained. "Why put the girl through the hacking off of her hair if there was no certainty?"

"Arghhh . . ." Clearly he expected women to be foolish like this. "It does not matter whether I am willing or not. We are at war. We do what we are told to do. I have orders to take her to Fort Lawrence, and I will comply. But I will be speaking to Mi'kmaq scouts along the way, asking them to notify Little Bear that we are planning an attack at *la Riviere St. Jean*. Then I must speak with Little Bear himself. At any point the Mi'kmaqs could become suspicious if they saw that a female is accompanying us. By the time they think it over, the chance to get Little Bear's help would be gone. If she were a squaw—a camp follower, as it were—we could get away with it. But this girl clearly is not. She is far too delicate, and very, very white."

"Dressed as a boy, she'll hardly be noticeable," Carrerot argued. "Her hair can be cut now, if you wish."

Stoically, Margaret kept her eyes on her feet, giving no indication that she understood the conversation. Her hair! Her beautiful hair! Granted, not beautiful just now, but....

The room was again silent.

Duval spat into the fireplace. "She is a woman, no matter how she dresses," he complained. "Invariably she will display herself, as all women do. Once my men see this, their concentration is broken."

"Since she wants desperately to get home again, she will do as we tell her. She will not display herself, if we warn her not to. She is far from stupid."

"She will have to undergo many rigors that will be difficult for her," Duval argued. "Such as sleeping on the ground, eating wild game, carrying packs. It's not all lakes and rivers. You know that."

"She must carry a pack?" Madame asked.

"Of course. All of us either carry packs or canoes when we portage. She would be very conspicuous if she did not. Or do you expect us to tote her around in a sedan chair?"

Oh, dear, Margaret thought. The sedan chair with curtains disappeared from her immediate future.

Duval leaned on the mantle. "*Merde*," he swore. For a time he was silent, and the Carrerots waited without trying to engage him. "Very well. We—my men and I—will carry the heavier loads. One of the packs can hold our sleeping robes, which aren't particularly heavy. She can carry that, I suppose, if she is sufficiently strong."

At least he was considering it!

"I'm sure she'll do whatever you wish, Marc, as long as the pack is sufficiently light and will accommodate her own bag with her personal items in it."

"What items?"

"Jeanne?" Carrerot, flustered, turned to his wife.

"Marc, she is a woman! Need you ask?"

"*Merde*," he swore again. "We will be under constant observation."

"She can take care of her needs under the cover of darkness, if necessary."

The room throbbed in the silence as he thought it over, staring at the hearth's andirons. It was safer to look at him now, and as Margaret did so, he looked up and directly at her. Not even a flicker of expression crossed his face, and his eyes showed no warmth.

"Scissors." He held out his hand.

"Yes. Here." Madame Carrerot handed them over.

"Move her in front of me. I wish to interrogate her while I cut her hair."

"Certainly."

LeBlanc tugged at Margaret's chair. "He wishes you to sit in front of him."

"He is going to cut my hair, isn't he?"

"*Oui*."

"It will look awful, *Monsieur* LeBlanc!"

"You had best cooperate, *Mademoiselle*. Much depends on it."

The chair now in place, she sat, motionless, as Duval pulled a piece of hair straight out from her head and cut it off.

"There! That was not so bad, was it?" His English was virtually unaccented. "They tell me you are Bostonian."

"Yes." She closed her eyes so no one would see the dampness gleaming in them as he picked up another lock of hair, cut it, moved slightly to her left, picked up another.

"Boston is the provincial capital of Massachusetts Bay Colony, is that not so?"

"Yes, it is."

"In what manner do you live there? Are you married? Do you live at home with your parents? Are you a servant?" Snip. Snip.

"I live at home," she answered. "With my parents." She shut her eyes tighter as she thought of Mama. Home, whenever or however she got there, would be quite different from her remembrance of it.

Snip. Snip. "Your father's occupation?"

"He is a clerk at a counting house," she lied. She'd decided on this falsehood between naps, and was ready with an instant reply.

Her ruse worked. Duval did not pursue the subject.

"If you come with me," he said, "you must do exactly what I tell you." Snip. Snip. He ran his fingers through her ruined hair, as though judging its length, nodded with apparent satisfaction, moved around behind her.

"I will do whatever I have to, sir."

He did not pause in his clipping, but sighed again. "She does not look strong," he said to Carrerot in French. "She looks puny."

"She IS puny!" Carrerot laughed. "She is a girl!"

And one accustomed to lifting heavy bolts of linen and wool off shelves and back again, she longed to tell them. She was stronger than she looked!

He moved around to the uncut side. Snip. Snip. Stood back, looking over the results. "You are now a boy," he announced, without humor. "The hat would be too warm in any case."

"She resembles a porcupine," Carrerot chortled. The others laughed.

Madame held up the jacket. Margaret shrugged into it. The sleeves were too long, but it would be warm. The cap stored in its pocket fit perfectly.

"It is fine," he said impatiently. "*C'est bien*. Get your pack, Miss Robinson, and follow me. Now."

CHAPTER FOUR

LeBlanc fetched it and handed it to her. "You heard him, *Mademoiselle. Bon voyage!* God be with you!"

Duval was already at the stairs, starting down, looking neither right nor left nor behind, to see if she were following. The street door opened, and as she hurried after him, he disappeared into the night.

"Wait!" she cried, but he did not. It was of no concern to him that her legs were not as long as his, that the boots were too large and the jacket too warm for the night air. Sweat was starting to stream down her face, stinging her eyes. She tripped, falling to her hands and knees.

"Wait, Mr. Duval!"

He did not.

There was a stitch in her side from running after him, and now there were scrapes on the palms of her hands that stung badly.

Margaret Roberge, she told herself, brushing off her hands and the knees of her leggings, picking up her pack, you will have to take whatever comes your way, without complaining. It's how you'll get home, and nothing else matters.

On the other side of the gate where there was a mass of huts and tents, a dory was drawn up onto the sand. Duval pushed it into the water without regard for his moccasins, gestured.

Apparently she was to wade in also. The water seeping into her boots was blessedly cool. She scrambled over the dory's side. "I thought we were going by canoe, Monsieur."

He made no response to this conversational gambit. Climbing in after her, he, seated himself and looked over his shoulder to line up his destination. The dory shot into the harbor. "See that little ship over there behind me?"

It was a small schooner, with sails already hoisted a quarter of the way up the mast.

Firmly she refused to allow herself to think of *L'Esperance de Dieu* or *Lady Nan*.

"Our canoes and packs are onboard already, and my men. The ship's captain will take us north, and then west, around the tip of *Île Royale*, which is where we are now. Then we will sail west and over to *Île St. Jean*, which is not far away. There we put the canoes in and paddle to the far side of a bay. Then we will portage to a river that runs to the Red Sea—the English call it Northumberland Strait—which we will cross to the mainland of Acadia where is the English Fort Lawrence. That is all I will tell you, *Mademoiselle*. From now on you will do what you are told, no questions asked."

I will never leave home again, she promised herself.

At the schooner, he threw her bag up onto the deck, climbed its rope ladder and reached for her, hauling her up and over the rail as though she, too, were a bag.

"Does the prisoner have a secure place to stay?" he asked the captain.

"In the galley," the fellow replied. "Cook will find something for him to do, and will keep an eye on him besides. He can sleep by the stove come night."

This does not bode well, she thought, as Duval pushed her toward the hatch.

"Go!"

"Up anchor!" the captain roared, and the deck was instantly filled with men ready to haul the sails up the rest of the way.

No one was watching and no one cared about her or the possibility of escape, for there was none. There was nowhere she could go but down into the bowels of the ship, to the galley, where she pretended to understand nothing that the cook said to her.

Following pantomimed instructions, she fed kindling to the pot-bellied stove, washed and wiped bowls and carried them to the adjacent cabin, empty save for a long table bolted to the floor. The men ate in shifts; the dishes and mugs and spoons were cleaned up after each, the table reset. After the third shift, which included Duval and his men, she finished up the washing, wiping, and stowing away of the dishes and pots, while the cook drank from a bottle with contentment, watching his work being done for him.

On deck, when finally she was free to climb up to it, the sun was still in the sky, though low, for in so northerly a latitude, a day approaching the summer solstice was nearly twice as long as night. Louisbourg lay a long way behind them, the scattered camp fires of the Acadians on knolls and high places looking like small stars in the approaching night. From the desultory remarks of the crew, she knew they did not expect bad weather, and was grateful. Duval would be incensed if he had to deal with a sea-sick female!

Tomorrow or the next day she would be in the wilderness with this rude and surly man, accompanied by a whole group of rude and surly men whom she had yet to distinguish from the sailors of the ship. Her position as a hostage would protect her from them to some degree, she hoped, for she would have to be alive and well when they delivered her to the English fort. But would she be molested at all? Fed well? Given decent sleeping quarters? How long would this round-about journey take?

Don't think about that, she told herself. Just play your part, and one day you'll be home. For now, let that thought be your north star.

But curled up by the galley's stove that night, wrapped in a blanket that did nothing to ease the hardness of the floor, she allowed slow tears to soak into the scratchy wool, and prayed to the God she knew so little about that Mama was safe, wherever she was, and that the trials that surely lay ahead would be surmountable, and that somehow she would get to Boston.

Soon, please!

CHAPTER

5

The Campfire

He disappeared, lithe as a leopard or a lion, sliding over one fallen tree trunk and under another. The men waited quietly, resting. Closing her eyes, Margaret rested too. The strain of being a hostage, along with shipwreck and losing Mama, was taking its toll. As well, she had not slept much since leaving Louisbourg.

At dawn today they had entered a bay on the north side of *Île St. Jean*. The canoes—three of them—were lowered into the water, filled with packs passing hand to hand down the ladder. The paddlers took their places; Margaret was tucked into Duval's canoe with such packs as could fit around her.

Then they entered the small bay, riding swiftly with the incoming tide. Pulling the canoes onto land, they waited. When Duval returned, it would be time to walk.

The men were eager to move on. Whatever Duval asked of them they gave. Their commitment to him was absolute.

Duval.

Confident. Sure of his prowess.

Disdainful. Angry.

His anger was not necessarily directed at her, she believed. But it surely included her, for it was an abiding, relentless force, driving all his actions. It caused him to look right past her, speaking to her only when he had to. But he had given permission for Armand St. Martin, his bow paddler, to talk with her quietly while they waited. St. Martin was the only member of the group, besides Duval, who spoke English.

"How long will we travel today?" she asked him.

"Until we reach the Red Sea. There is a river nearby. We will ride upon it until late afternoon. Then we arrive."

"Why has Mr. Duval left us?" she asked.

"He consults with the Mi'kmaq scouts. This land is theirs. We do not move upon it without their consent. Also, he wishes them to notify their Sachem—Little Bear—that we are coming. And also to find out if the British warship still blockades *la Riviere St. Jean*."

"There is a warship here? On this island?"

"No!" he laughed. "*La Riviere St. Jean* is south of us. Not far from the Maine territory."

"Saint John must be a French favorite, since he has so many places named after him."

"That is so, *Mademoiselle*. We also celebrate him at the summer solstice with a feast day."

"Are you Acadian, Armand?"

"I am." He said it with pride. "I was born at Grand Pré, my father and mother have a farm there and my brothers help them with it while I follow Duval."

"Follow him where?"

"To war, *Mademoiselle*. To war with your countrymen."

She watched him whittle a whistle. "The Mi'kmaq children enjoy these," he explained.

"How nice," she said, without caring. "I am tired, *Monsieur* St. Martin. How far away is the river?"

"Some distance, I fear," he apologized. "Also, I wish you would call me Armand. After all, we have been travelling two nights and two days in the same vessel. Surely we need not the formality."

"Then, I am Marguerite." The French pronunciation of her name.

"*Bien.*" Good.

The bushes whipped about as Duval reappeared. "All is in order," he called in French. "The English are hiding behind the walls of their fort. The British ship still guards the mouth of the *la Riviere St. Jean.* Members of Little Bear's council will meet with us tonight. *Allons!*"

Quickly he moved to his canoe, kneeling and tipping it over his head, rising up with it balanced on his shoulders. The other stern paddlers followed suit while the bow paddlers picked up the packs, two for each, and slung them over their shoulders. Only hers was left, containing her personal things and several sleeping robes. It had been placed on a nearby boulder at shoulder height so that she could easily slide into its straps. This she did, edged it off the boulder and promptly fell backwards.

"Her pack appears to be too heavy, Marc. She has fallen over," Armand told him from beneath his load.

Duval crouched, moved out from under his canoe, laid it carefully on the ground. Coming over to her, he waited until she slid free of her pack. "I should never have let you come." His voice was quiet, deadly with his scorn. "On your feet. Try again."

"I'm sorry, *Monsieur*—"

"Kindly shut your mouth," he snarled, "lest the Mi'kmaqs hear your female voice. Get into the straps. I will hold the pack until you have balanced it."

He shifted it one way and then the other as she slipped her arms into the bindings and bent forward far enough to take its weight.

"*Bien.* Get in line, behind me and in front of St. Martin." He returned to his canoe and again hoisted it into place. The line moved forward. Armand reached out and lifted the weight of her pack. Duval, his head under his canoe, could not see this assistance, nor could the stern paddler following Armand, carrying his own canoe and unable to see anything but his feet and the ground upon which he trod.

Everyone seemed sure-footed as they marched along the nearly hidden trail, nothing more than a firmness underfoot, yet the men knew exactly where to place their feet, pushing aside bushy branches with flowers on them, and multitudes of other twiggy, snarly growing things.

It was endless. Despite Armand behind, taking much of her pack's weight and propelling her forward, it was a merciless journey. On and on, one foot after the other, all of the pack carriers bent over like old people without even a walking stick.

She had prided herself on her strength and agility, accustomed to being on her feet at the store. But this! This was simply a matter of endurance, sweating under the sun as it rose to its zenith. Then a river appeared, rising up in the middle of the wilderness. Without discussion, the canoes were put back in the water, packs replaced, Margaret wedged into her own space in Duval's boat. At his quiet command, the canoes were launched. The current was with them, and they flew downstream as the afternoon progressed until there was a sea-breeze, blessedly cool, and they arrived at the Northumberland Strait. The sun was low on the horizon as they pulled ashore.

Duval turned to his men. "Little Bear's scouts tell me that some of his council members will meet with us tonight. We will smoke with them, and ask their advice—which, as you know, they love giving—about the taking of the warship. They will also tell Little Bear when we think we will arrive tomorrow."

"How is it that this ship cannot just sail into the river and take the French one?" asked Pierre.

"It is too big to negotiate the reversing falls. By now the French cargo is unloaded, *naturellement*. Guns and bullets and knives and hatchets. The problem is that it cannot get past the warship and return to Quebec City. So we shall take the warship ourselves, opening the way. The men at our fort will fire on the ship while we board it and capture it."

"What fort?" Margaret whispered to Armand.

"It is called Menagoueche," he answered. "Small, but has a cannon which will cause a diversion."

"And you believe Little Bear will send men to help us?" one of the men asked Duval.

"The scouts seem to think so. Little Bear has made summer camp in his customary place." He gestured toward the strait, the far shore of which could not be seen. "As soon as we get to him, Pierre and Gaston, Robert and Yves, will depart for Grand Pré and notify the Acadians of our plan. As many as are able will accompany them to *la Riviere St. Jean*. Bonsoleil and his men are there already. Armand and I will deliver the girl to Fort Lawrence and fetch Paul-Henri. We will join you at St. John, and all of us will be ready to march into Maine Territory when the fleet arrives to bombard the coastal settlements and trading posts."

Maine! The Fleet! Good God, was there no end?

"Marc," Armand protested. "We do not truly know that the fleet is coming."

"Of course we do!" he retorted. "Father LeLoutre went to France himself this past winter, to request it. Believe me, the ships will be coming up over the horizon any day now. You must not allow any doubt about this to enter your mind, especially when you are speaking to the Acadians. They must not be allowed to doubt either. If they do, they will start debating and then they will argue about it, and they'll forget that we are at war with the English because they'll be too busy disagreeing with each other. You know that."

They sounded quite provincial, these Acadians. But they had been isolated here for a long time, Margaret remembered, without seeing or talking to anyone other than themselves. That would make anybody provincial, let alone farmers who probably couldn't read or write.

The canoes were pulled up to the edge of the woods. Two of them were propped up with sticks, providing a safe haven for the packs. Armand propped up the third, foraged for moss, chopping off the fragrant tips of hemlock, spreading the soft mass under the canoe. Removing a pelt from her pack, he covered everything, then bowed with a sweeping gesture.

"*Chez vous!*" he grinned proudly, happy to provide for her comfort.

"Where will you sleep?" she asked.

"Nearby, *Mademoiselle*, so you need not worry that an animal will molest you. I, Armand St. Martin, will never let that happen!"

"Thank you," she sighed, crawling under the canoe and sinking down on the pelt. Armand's mound of fir tips and moss were soft and clean-smelling. Lying on them was paradise; he brought a blue blanket from one of the packs to use as a cover. Soon she was snug, relaxed, listening to the calls of birds echoing through the woods while the voices of the men grew distant . . . distant . . .

Evening. The smell of roasting rabbit woke her, and the fragrance of tea.

"*Mademoiselle!*" It was Armand, gently shaking her. "Arise *Mademoiselle*. It is time to eat."

Rubbing sleep from her eyes, she crawled out from under her canoe and got to her feet. He was holding a shallow wooden bowl from which steam arose. Tea! Where had it come from! Gratefully she took it, drank and looked around at the encampment. Rabbits were roasting on green sticks, along with some fish from the river. The men sat around the fire, smoking and drinking, also from bowls. Somehow, she did not believe their beverage was tea.

Armand folded up her sleeping robe and stuffed it back into her pack. Spreading out the blue cloth, he gestured for her to sit, then seated himself companionably beside her.

"There is a little time before the rabbits are done. Let us share companionship now. Later we will be visited, and there will be no opportunity."

"Visited!" She must, at all cost, feign ignorance lest they realize she understood French. She could not know that Little Bear's men were coming. "Who?"

"Friends of Marc Duval. But they will not be here until later. Nearly dark." His eyes roamed over her face. "You are English, yes?"

"My mother was."

"I was sorry to hear about her."

Margaret nodded, not trusting herself to speak.

"Yet you have not blue eyes, such as *les Anglais* do."

"My father is Italian," she lied. "Italians are dark, like French people are."

"Italians."

"They come from Italy. Do you know where that is, Armand?"

"No, *Mademoiselle*," he confessed humbly.

"Italy, where Italians live, is near France."

"Ah," he breathed. "Across the great sea."

"There are all kinds of people in the English colonies. Catholics in Maryland. Jews in New York, and Dutch. Germans and Welsh in Pennsylvania."

He shook his head, unable to understand.

"We often deal with the *Bostonais*," he offered, "when we are not at war with them. These others, do they trade with the *Bostonais* also?"

"Yes." When we can get away with it, she did not add. Intercolonial trade was not encouraged by the crown.

"Would they make jewelry to sell?"

"Of course! Very beautiful jewelry."

"Perhaps things that would interest the Mi'kmaqs. Trinkets, perhaps, such as we have not yet seen. Different tools," Armand mused. "That would be good for our brotherhood."

"Your brotherhood?"

"Our brotherhood with the Mi'kmaqs. They will remain loyal to us, but when we give them the cloth and the ribbons, that is better. And new things? That would be good. They value most that which they do not have, the Mi'kmaqs, just as we do. They are like all people in many ways."

"I should hope not!" she retorted. "I have heard some very unpleasant things about the Indians. They are ungodly and without manners of any kind, and untrustworthy."

"Marc is very trustworthy," Armand answered back. "And he is a good leader, besides."

"Marc Duval? He is an Indian?"

"His mother was of the Malacite Nation, from Maine."

"A half-breed?" She had heard nothing but evil about these depraved beings. A rising of distaste filled her awareness.

"We do not call them half-breeds," Armand said uncomfortably. "The Indians, they are one with us in the Lord Jesus. The Jesuits have converted many of them."

"They are drunkards."

"Mademoiselle, *sans doute* the English—your people—give them the alcohol, and encourage them to get drunk." Armand protested. "The French do not. The native, he cannot drink much without needing more, and more. But not Marc Duval! He drinks better than we Acadians do!" Proudly, Armand nodded. "And since he is also Malacite—The People of the Dawn, as they say—the Mi'kmaqs, trust him, for they, too, are People of the Dawn."

As though he could hear, Duval suddenly looked up from the campfire. "If you're through with your dallying, Armand," he called in French, "perhaps you would be so kind as to join us at the fire?"

"*Plus tard, peut-être?*" Armand called back. Perhaps later?

Duval rose in a fluid motion, came over to them. "Tell me, does that blue cloth come from our bag of gifts?"

Armand jumped up, looking abashed and even ashamed. "Yes, Marc. It does. I believed *Mademoiselle* would enjoy resting upon it."

"*Mademoiselle* is a boy, you oaf. Would you give a boy a pretty cloth to sit upon, for God's sake?"

"You are right, Marc. I quite forgot."

"It is done now." Duval shrugged.

"Must you take him away, Mr. Duval?" Margaret protested. "I am learning so much by talking with him."

"He cannot help himself, hoping to gain your admiration, *Mademoiselle*. He is most likely saying more than he should." He eyed the short, bristling dark hair framing her face, glanced at the shapeless tunic and drooping leggins. "You look like a beggar, it is true. But you are a woman and my men are well aware of it."

"Actually, she is quite lovely, *n'est ce pas?*" Armand smiled gently.

"It is true. Even looking as you do, *Mademoiselle* Robinson, we are all aware of your charms."

Although aching and stiff, she rose and straightened her shoulders. "I do not need the compliments of a half-breed," she said in the coldest voice she could contrive. "You will desist, *Monsieur* Duval."

There was a moment of shocked silence. A squirrel chuckled from a nearby tree.

Rage filled his eyes. "What did you tell her, Armand?" he asked, watching her.

"Has she said something offensive?" Armand asked, consternation clear in his voice.

"She calls me a half-breed."

Armand softly groaned. "Please accept my apology, Marc. It is all my fault. I told her why the Mi'kmaqs trust you. How it is that you are their brother."

"Apology accepted," Duval said curtly. "You will stay here, Miss Robinson. When we are finished with our meal, we will bring you what is left over." He turned away. "Armand, get rid of the fucking blanket. Then come eat a rabbit."

Without even a glance they left her, Duval joining the others, Armand quickly stuffing the blanket beneath the sleeping robe and hurrying over to the fire. Margaret sat in front of her canoe shelter until Armand gathered what scraps were left and brought them to her.

"Your dinner, *Mademoiselle*."

"Armand!" she said softly. "I should not have called him a half-breed."

"No," he agreed. "You should not have done so."

"Would you tell him that I am sorry?"

"No. Duval has suffered much at the hands of the English people. They have caused him great bitterness. I will say nothing more that reminds him of it."

He turned away, and it was as though all possibility of hope went with him. She had alienated the one person willing to befriend her.

The long Acadian twilight set in as she picked at rabbit remnants and flakes of fish. It was nearly dark when Duval snapped

CHAPTER FIVE

his fingers to get her attention, pointed to a stunted tree some twenty feet from the fire. "Sit there with your legs crossed, as a boy would do, and stay until I tell you otherwise."

He spoke to Pierre without waiting to find out if she would obey him. "Sit between her and the fire. She will be unobtrusive that way. I will tell our visitors that you promised your sister, the urchin's mother, to stay by him at all times. Do it now. They are near."

No visitors were apparent, but she was learning that Duval had ways of knowing these things. Moving over to the tree, she crossed her legs as he'd instructed. In this unladylike position, she was not fully covered. Desperately she shifted her tunic this way and that, and by rucking it up higher, found there was enough extra material to tuck between her legs.

Pierre settled himself as Duval instructed. At the fire, surrounded by its ring of stones, Robert and Gaston sat on one side of Duval, Armand and Yves the other. Everyone waited quietly, waited, waited, until three natives stepped soundlessly from the woods.

They were ugly. Their faces were broad and flat, their noses blunt, their hair rough and dull. But clean shaven and well-built. Their clothing was a mixture of European shirts and animal hide leggings, stained and filthy. But if they looked like beggars, they obviously did not feel like ones as they squatted opposite Duval and his men.

Pierre reached back, behind himself, and clasped her knee, carressed it lightly with his thumb.

Duval retrieved tobacco and a pipe from a cranny she could not see. Lighting it, he passed it to the Mi'kmaqs who passed it back after deeply inhaling. Marc's men smoked it, passed it over, back and forth while Duval spoke clearly, though incomprehensibly, in their language.

Pierre's hand moved up.

The Mi'kmaqs stretched out on the ground, thinking over what they had been told while Duval and his men patiently watched and smoked.

Pierre's hand slowly worked its way toward her woman-place.

"Stop right now, Pierre," she said in icy French, her voice carrying distinctly in the evening stillness. *Arretez dés maintenant.*

Pierre quickly withdrew his hand. At the fire the reclining Mi'kmaqs sat up, looking to Duval. He laughed, said something that made them laugh, too. Then the contents of one of the packs was spread out on the ground to admire. More tobacco was smoked. The Mi'kmaqs took what gifts they wanted and then drifted away toward the edge of the clearing, and were gone as though they had simply melted on the spot and seeped into the ground.

And Margaret Roberge was left with six renegades who now knew she had understood everything that had been said, from the first day to this.

"Bring her to the fire," Duval said and the man Pierre reached for her.

"Don't you ever touch me!" With as much dignity as she could muster, she rose in one motion as she had seen Duval do. Keeping her distance from Pierre, she went around to the far side of the fire where the Indians had sat, lain, smoked, and knelt down. Duval looked her over.

He is only a half breed, she told herself. He is inferior to you. Look him in the eye and keep your head high.

Yet he was in control, and she was not.

"Did I hear you correctly?" he asked in French.

"*Oui.*" She took a deep breath. "*Vous avez entendu correctement.*" You have heard correctly.

His face was lit by the glowing coals. He shoved them about with a small stick. "Thus you know we plan to capture the English

CHAPTER FIVE

ship at *La Riviére St. Jean*. You know that Father LeLoutre has requested the French fleet. You know we will attack the territory of Maine and take back the land stolen from us. What else do you know?"

"That we are going to Fort Lawrence where I will be exchanged for your man Paul-Henri," she said with a tremor in her voice that she could not control.

Duval glanced at his comrades, who watched, coiled like snakes and ready. For what?

She waited.

"Oh, *merde*," he said to them.

The men mumbled among themselves, but knowing she could understand, kept their voices low.

"So, you are French," Duval observed. *Tu es Francais*.

"In a manner of speaking."

"And what manner is that?"

"I am descended from French Protestants. They are called Huguenots. Some of them fled France when so many were massacred on St. Bartholomew's Day, a long time ago. Until very recently, the Huguenot church was active in Boston, and French was spoken there and in all our homes. Which is why I am so familiar with your language."

"Robinson is an English name."

"Yes."

"Is it your name?"

"No," she sighed. "I am Roberge. I had to change to Robinson, *Monsieur*. It would have been difficult, I thought—confusing, to say the least, to present the captain of *L'Esperance de Dieu* with my true name, which is indeed French."

He stared at her. "I'll be damned," he said eventually. *Que je sois damné*.

"She is clever, is she not?" Pierre sneered.

"Not bad looking, either," remarked Robert.

"*Elle est Francaise*," Gaston pointed out. "What else would you expect?"

"Not really French. Just playing at it."

"I think she should be punished."

"Truly, I agree. She has deceived us."

"I think..."

"That man tried to touch me," she said quickly, pointing at Pierre before their opinions could become lethal. "I would appreciate it if such a thing did not occur again."

"Since you have understood everything, you also understand that Pierre will be leaving us after we reach Little Bear's camp tomorrow, is that not so?"

"Well, yes."

"Thus he will have no further opportunity to bother you."

"But this night is still young," Pierre snorted with suppressed laughter and mounting excitement. The others laughed, too, their voices low and throaty with rising lust.

She was at their mercy. Across from her, Duval watched, elbow on knee, chin in hand.

"Please!" she cried, her voice shaking and thin. "It is not my fault that I know French. It is not my fault that you spoke indiscriminately. Why should I be punished for that?"

"It is often the fate of the enemy. And you are English."

"I am American!" she cried. "There are many Americans who do not like the English, either!"

"And many who do." Idly, as though time were unimportant to him, Duval picked up a twig and placed it on the dying coals, then another and another until a flame jumped up, and addressed his men. "We must move fast, for once she is exchanged she will tell the Commander about our plan to take the warship."

"Certainly she will tell!"

"She is no better than a spy."

"Perhaps she is a spy."

"Let's make her pay!"

"Give us our chance, Duval!" Robert shouted. "Fair is fair!"

"Yes!" The others chorused. "Yes!"

In a motion too quick to follow, Duval reached across the flame and took Margaret's wrist in a grip of iron as though he would draw her arm into the fire. Yet he did not.

"Tell us you are not a spy, *Mademoiselle*," he said in French. His grip on her wrist did not falter, even when the sleeve of his tunic began to smoke.

"I am not a spy, *Monsieur* Duval!"

"And what did you plan to do with the information we have inadvertently given you?"

"I have no plan. No plan at all. I just want to go home. Mr. Duval! Please! Let me go! Move your arm! You will be burned!"

She tried to draw away, but could do nothing in his grasp. The cloth of his tunic ignited with tongues of flame, and the hairs on his arm shriveled up, snapping.

"I am going to ask you a question in English, so my men will not understand."

"Please!" she wept. "Take your arm from the fire!"

"Answer me, *Mademoiselle*. In English. With this pause, they will be diverted. Tell me, in English, why you were going to London."

"To meet my father's business contacts."

"A clerk has business in *Londres?*"

"I lied about that. I will explain. Please remove your arm!"

"Very well." Without hurrying, he released her wrist, watching her closely. At so close a range as this, there should have been evidence of pain in his eyes. But there was not. He turned to his men, paying no heed to his wounded arm. "Soon, we'll have Paul-Henri, who will be free to help us take Maine, restore the land of the Malacite and the Acadian. Soon, the fleet will arrive to cover our attack. It won't matter what the girl knows. What will matter is that we take the ship at St. Jean, that we march south to Maine Territory, and that we attack. And drive the English out!"

His voice was vibrant, ringing out over the Red Sea.

"Yes! Yes!"

He leaped to his feet. "Soon all Acadia will be one again!"

"Yes!"

"And it will be French again."

"Yes! Yes!" All of them were on their feet now. "Yes!"

"Are you ready?"

"Yes! Yes!"

"Then let us dive into the sea and refresh ourselves, cleanse ourselves, sleep and be ready to leave at dawn. Little Bear's summer camp is directly across from us. We will reach it by midday, and disburse according to plan. Come!"

Mesmerized, they followed him to the water, throwing their garments on the sand and diving in.

She was not so foolish as to waste the opportunity. She slipped under her canoe-shelter and changed the angle of the stick so that it was lower to the ground, the better to hide. After an interminable wait she heard them return, laughing and swatting each other with their discarded clothes. They dispersed, rolled up in the sleeping robes. Duval banked the fire, flung his robe over his shoulders and sat vigil in front of her canoe's tilted shelter.

She spoke quietly. "What did you tell the Indians? How did you explain me?"

"I said that you are my woman, but I wished to disguise you so that none of Little Bear's men would ravish you. But that Pierre could not control himself."

"And they laughed."

"They did. They observed that my own men were more of a hazard than Little Bear's."

"And the Indians? Would they have molested me?"

"Who knows, Miss Robinson? Kidnap is more likely. An extra squaw is always welcome. Sleep now. Dawn comes early."

"I will try. Good night."

"Good night."

His woman. He told them she was his woman.

For whom he allowed himself to be burned, distracting his men. Whom he would deliver to Fort Lawrence soon. To be exchanged, returned to Boston, to be united in marriage with Robert Blake, hopefully to own Roberge Imports....

The sleepless summer night passed.

CHAPTER

6

The Bath

Began the early dawn.
A squadron of ducks flew low overhead, their feathers whistling. Birds rose up from the bushes and settled again, fussing and feeding; shafts of sun, tentative at first and then more fearless, crept silently, swiftly along the shore, blessing each dwelling as it went.

The village did not stir. From the doorway of the tipi secured for her use, Margaret peered out at the cluster of other tipi's that made up Little Bear's summer camp. To prevent her being found out, Duval had asked for one just for her use, and so she had spent the whole long evening and night by herself in this miserable place, batting at bugs and itching in the night dampness, thinking malevolent thoughts. They had crossed the Strait and found the mouth of a river where Little Bear's tribe camped. The men unpacked their goods, spread them out along the stream, then got back in their canoes and paddled upriver into the wilderness, taking Armand with them.

Armand? He was supposed to accompany Duval and herself to Fort Lawrence!

During the evening, Duval himself had brought her some inedible food and had informed her that they could leave this morning, if that was her desire.

Desire! She couldn't get away from here fast enough!

"What I also desire is to know why Armand has left."

"He will be taken to this river's source—where it arises. He will hike to Fort Lawrence. You and I will also go to the source and hike to the Fort, but at a pace more comfortable for you. Armand will begin negotiations for Paul-Henri while waiting for us. If the English are agreeable, the exchange will be quick and the three of us, Armand, Paul-Henri and I, will be able to join the others at St. Jean before it is too late to be of use. You, of course, will go to Boston. Just now, *Mademoiselle*, I go to Little Bear, and arrange for his part in the attack on the English warship. I shall fetch you in the morning."

They had talked and then feasted late, the Mi'kmaqs and Duval. She had watched them from her tipi, watched the gifts being given, sealing the friendship between the tribe and the great French King across the waters. Judging by the affability around the campfire, an agreement must have been reached about aiding the Acadians in capturing the British warship.

Then the council broke up. Duval went off somewhere for the night and the village had fallen quickly silent, only the snapping and popping of the dying central fire breaking the forest stillness. No one had bothered her, or bothered about her. No one had looked her way or evinced curiosity about her. She was Duval's business, apparently, and whatever he wanted done—or not done—in her regard would be observed.

The sun was climbing higher, but still nothing stirred in the camp. Apparently the Indians had no particular place to go and no pressing reason for going there. Looking up at the dome of her tent, she watched clouds wandering slowly past the smoke hole. Finally a dog barked. A baby cried. Women's voices rose, fires were kindled.

The buckskin that served as a door was pulled aside, and Duval crawled in.

"*Bonjour.*" He sat companionably beside her, as though he had not maligned and belittled her ever since he'd first seen her. "Did you sleep at all?"

"A little."

His arm was covered with blisters. "I don't understand. Why did you do it?"

"You know not how close you were to being raped," he said.

"I guessed."

"You are a brave girl, Marguerite Roberge," he smiled slowly, using the French derivation of her name. "You kept your composure. You explained yourself well, even under pressure, so that I could understand how your deception came to be, and you let me handle the men in my own way. With a trial by fire, the moment of danger passed, and my control over them was absolute. And I discovered a great deal about you, Miss Robinson-Roberge. I found that you would not let me fry!"

"How long would you have continued—holding your arm over the fire?"

"For as long as it took to show the men that I was in control. Of you. Of them."

"Monsieur Duval, I hardly know what to say. It seems like such a hard thing to do."

"A deep part of Indian culture, *Mademoiselle*, is the ability to suffer. To withstand pain. I have learned these lessons well. Pain I can handle, for a deep part of me is Indian. Perhaps you have forgotten."

"I . . . I haven't forgotten."

"I must be able to do the things Indians do, if I am to be respected by them. I must be able to undergo suffering as the Mi'kmaqs do, for this is the measure of manhood—this and the ability to hunt. For the Indian female, she also is admired in proportion to her ability to shoulder pain. She dances during labor and sings during childbirth in just the same manner—and for the same reasons—that men chant tribal songs while dying by ritual torture."

She shuddered at the thought of torture, but he paid no attention.

"And because I am accepted as an equal, I can negotiate with the Mi'kmaqs, and my leadership both among my men and with the French is assured. Today you and I shall follow Pierre and Gaston and Armand, make our way to the source of the river. Our canoe is ready. I've brought some food along for you to eat as we travel. Come now."

Stuffing her sleeping robe into her pack, she crawled out, her cap low over her brow, head down, shoulders slumped so that no suggestion of her figure would show. The launch site was half a mile from the camp. The whole tribe had gathered on the bank, happily laughing and calling to one another. At their head stood Little Bear, his feathers impressive, his bear claw necklace polished. Long strings of wampum were looped like chains at his belt and a new hatchet hung there, too, its iron blade glistening in the sun. Beside him stood a young woman wrapped in a length of new red cloth. Ribbons were woven into her braids; her face was impassive as she stared at the hostage who limped behind Duval.

Their canoe waited. Margaret threw her pack in and grasped the far edge, preparing to climb up and over. Little Bear, wading in with Duval's pack—a small one but much larger than hers—boosted her up. He made a quiet comment as Duval hoisted himself in and they both laughed. Then removing his bear claw necklace, Little Bear reached over to drape it around Duval's neck. The watching tribe raised a murmur of approval. Pushing the canoe into the middle of the river, the sachem went back to his place on the bank, beside the girl.

She had eyes only for Duval. As the canoe was engaged by the current, he dipped in his paddle and pulled slowly, preventing it from drifting downstream. The girl stepped in front of Little Bear. In her own language she began to sing loudly above the sound of the river, and there with the whole tribe to watch, slowly unwrapped the red cloth covering her. Her pert beasts gleamed with grease, the nipples painted a startling red to match the cloth which slowly fell to her feet. Her singing grew louder as the canoe began to move upriver. Her hands rose to her breasts, which she held out as though inviting a man's touch, reminding her lover of the welcome he might expect when he visited her next time. She was still singing as Duval dug the paddle deep and the canoe moved around the nearest bend and the gathered tribe disappeared.

"No doubt you think Red Bird's performance is depraved," he said finally, when their progress was well established. "But she is only an Indian, is that not so? You must make allowance for her uncultured ways."

Margaret watched a submerged branch pass beneath the canoe; a small rushing waterfall made a rejoinder unnecessary. Surely he had known the nakedness of this Bird intimately. They had, surely, coupled only last night. What was there to say?

"Probably you thought Red Bird was—what is the word—overly—overly dramatic?" he persisted.

"Her message was clear enough, in any case." Again she imagined him making love to the girl—a surprisingly unwelcomed image that she pushed aside. "Do you pay for her favor?" she asked nastily.

"I gave her a gift to match her name. A whole bolt of red cloth, as you saw. My gift tells her that she pleases me and regardless of that which occurs or does not occur between us, the balance is achieved. I will be welcomed by her the next time I pass through."

"She will be waiting?"

"That remains her choice, with which I comply. An Indian maiden is always free to make her choice. No one ever forces her."

"An admirable arrangement."

"Red Bird is an admirable woman, flying free in pursuit of that which is important to her, and brings joy to those who watch."

"Until she marries?"

"She has responsibilities then, of course. But if she is dissatisfied, she can divorce her husband whenever she chooses to."

"What about her children?"

"Once they reach six years, the whole village takes care of them, and the mother is free."

The river ran a little slower. Hunger began to gnaw. "I would enjoy some breakfast, please."

"Yes, of course. It's on the top of the items in my pack. Untie the lashings—that's it."

Breakfast consisted of smoked, shriveled venison—far from satisfying, but better than nothing. She chewed at it and washed it down with cupped handfuls of river water, studying the bearded trees that reached out and over them.

The canoe veered quickly around a submerged boulder, then resumed its course.

"We take life as it comes to us," Duval said, as though the conversation had not been interrupted. "Thus Red Bird takes each day as it comes. She will not worry about whether she will like it. A lesson from which the English might well profit, since they are a continually worried race. They do not know how to grasp the present. They do not avail themselves of joy. They worry about morality constantly, yet are immoral."

"You have a low opinion of the English, Monsieur Duval."

"I do. They deserve it. They are stupid. There is much the English might learn from us, *Mademoiselle*, especially about waging war in the woods. For you, this small excursion can be a wonderful opportunity to learn how to live fully, should you choose to do so. For despite your French heritage, you are English by upbringing, and probably Puritanical. You most likely have never learned to enjoy anything. Now you can."

"We Huguenots are not Puritans. Calvinists, yes. Protestants, most certainly. But we are well able to enjoy life."

"Do you deny the Puritan influence?"

"No, I do not, Mr. Duval. It permeates Boston and all of New England. But how it affects those of us who live there is different for each person."

"I am happy to hear it, *Mademoiselle*. I would be sad to think you had never known joy."

She opened her mouth to reply, then realized she did not know what to say. Her moment of greatest joy was her last afternoon with Tyler Moore and the passion they had shared. Forbidden passion. Unrequited. And ultimately, not happy, but painful. She would not think about it. Instead, she would watch the heartland of Acadia passing slowly by. The trees were larger here than any she had seen before; along the shore and in the woods boulders were scattered, and many lay beneath the water, waiting to snag the canoe.

The rumbling came on them suddenly; around a bend, the water suddenly rushed toward them through countless waterfalls and chutes, deadly and swift, tumbling as far as the eye could see.

Duval pulled over. "Another stream meets this one above the turbulence. We'll portage through the woods and rejoin our river above it," he said. "I'll carry the canoe and take it to the put-in point. Follow me, if you please."

He handed her the pack with her personal things.

"The path is well trodden, and there is a clearing halfway along it, with a small stream and a little pool. Quite well screened by trees—an ideal spot in which to bathe, if the thought appeals to you, Miss Roberge." His eyes held hers. "At the other end of the path, the canoe will await you."

To bathe! To be clean, fresh, to wear the extra chemise in her pack next to her skin—yes, that would be good. Although regular bathing was not an absolute requirement in colonial society, no city bred woman ever, ever smelled this bad, nor had so dirty a face!

Duval settled his pack, tipped the canoe and hoisted it upon his shoulders. *"Allons!"* he called, and set off.

Tucking the strap of her own pack over one shoulder, she followed, picking her way carefully around exposed roots and sharp stones until the trail smoothed out a bit and led to the small clearing Duval had described, where a stream fed a shimmering pool. From here the roaring of the white water was a muffled grumble, as though an argument were being carried on in the distance. Shafts of sunlight fell to the forest floor; insects sailed in them, and the very air was scented with the pine and verdant earth. In the overhanging branches of an oak tree, birds hopped and squirrels skittered, their comings and goings amplifying the silent listening of the wilderness.

Margaret listened, too, breathed deeply. Tension left her as she absorbed the peaceful stillness of the woods.

"I will continue on to the end, where the path meets the river, and wait for you there," Duval said from under the canoe. "Enjoy yourself, *Mademoiselle.*"

CHAPTER SIX

The verdant woods swallowed him up.
Should she do it?
Did she dare?
Yes!

Quickly she peeled off her boots, the leggins, the tunic, the short gown. Taking her bath sponge from her pack, she dipped it in the pool and scrubbed herself swiftly, briskly; the fresh, clean air of the woods touched all of her, all at once, the pure warmth of the sun fell cleanly on her like the caress of a weightless hand. Expanding under such unaccustomed sensuality, she waded deeper into the pool and slowly sank, gasping as the cold water clutched at her and then released her into a cool embrace. She submerged her face, her bristly hair, let the magic of the place have its way with her ...

Scrubbing at her scalp, feeling it tingle—no longer hampered by long hair—she stretched out and floated and kicked like a child. Water sprayed everywhere into the sunshine, twinkling, rainbowed.

There was a distant crackling. Was Duval coming? Notifying her by breaking a stick that he was near? But he had said he would wait!

She clambered out, panic stricken. She must quickly put on her filthy tunic—but it was gone.

Her boots and leggings too, and the pack itself.

The woods slumbered silently now, the birds waiting. No branches and no twigs broke under the foot of any man or beast. It must have been a startled deer, she thought ... or a rabbit ....

"Looking for something, Miss Roberge?"

He was suddenly there before her, admiration written on his face, his eyes intense. He was not an impassive half-breed. He had no need to impress his followers. The embittered leader of rebels was gone, and here was simply a man delighting in the loveliness of a woman.

And here was a woman, wringing wet, without a stitch to cover herself. In the most feminine of female instincts, she tried to shield her breasts and crotch.

"You have lost your clothes, *Mademoiselle?*"

She looked up and saw that he was smiling.

"I think you have taken them, and I would like to have them back." Her heart in her throat hammered and deafened her. "Now."

"I am only answering your need, Marguerite Roberge," he said, his eyes on her mouth, reaching out a hand to caress her. "For you have had an abundance of time in which to refresh yourself. That you have not already got your clothes on tells me that you were waiting for me."

She looked away. "Truly I was not. It was only that the sun—the air—felt so good . . ." She stopped. This was a ridiculous conversation, being held under impossible circumstances.

"On the skin? Indeed, it does feel good. It is one of life's supreme pleasures—which few Europeans even know about." Then he moved in, gently pinning her hands behind her. He bent to kiss her breasts, one and then the other, and his dark hair brushed her skin and his mouth was tender, his lips soft against the softness of her flesh. Without her knowing it would happen, her whole body answered, opening, glowing . . . . Her breath caught in her throat as his lips moved up, and she was ready when his mouth found hers. He kissed her without hurrying, as though waiting for her to meet him, and within her was a surging—a need for more.

Stepping back, he watched her with the sureness of a man who knew how to satisfy a woman. "Behind that tree—" he tipped his head toward it—"you will find a bundle. Avail yourself of its contents. I will wait for you at the river."

Then he was gone. Indeed, on the other side of the tree was a bundle wrapped in the blue blanket Armand had given her.

Doeskin leggings, a sleeveless tunic that fell mid-thigh, beaded moccasins, and, and—

A breech clout. A breech clout! Men wore those! And older boys. She had seen them at Little Bear's camp. Puzzled, she held it up, saw that it was quite narrow, just wide enough to cover the exposed place that leggings left bare and long enough to hang free in front and behind from a rawhide strap that would tie around her waist.

She tried it. Soft. Very soft in the center, firmer as it was folded under and over the strap and left to dangle.

A sleeveless vest, fringed leggins, soft doeskin moccasins followed, and then she was ready. Huh. No longer would she have to worry about sitting cross legged!

She looked around the clearing again, at the pool and stream quiet and sparkling, and the sun falling to the earth. She lingered. Besides the peace of the forest, something else filled her, something for which she had no name, something that frightened and elated her, and left her breathless—

She picked up the blue blanket. Where had her second set of clothes gotten to? No matter. She must move on. Regretfully she followed the path, but she inhabited an unreal world as she did so, a world full of elation and confusion, a world suspended somewhere between this moment and the next. One she had not known about before, nor believed existed; one which showed her without a shadow of doubt that she had never loved Tyler Moore or anyone else. That she had never in her life known about love between a man and a woman.

And now, perhaps, she had a chance to learn.

CHAPTER

7

The Pagan

He was waiting. The river was narrower and flowed more slowly here, at this end of the portage. She climbed into the canoe and they started off again. There was no conversation between them as once again the woods passed by, with Princess Margaret in her floating sedan chair taking it all in. The forest was a living, breathing being that watched as she passed.

When the canoe scraped very gently against the bottom of the stream bed, the sun was low. There was a long silence.

"We will camp here, and start off early in the morning."

Here? They would sleep here? She was paralyzed with fear, with passion, with confusion.

"Do you like your new clothes? I am hopeful you will find them comfortable for travel."

"Indeed, I thank you. Where are my old ones?"

"Buried. The clean ones are in your pack, and your sleeping robe."

"Some animal will dig the old ones up, I'm sure. Thinking there's a carcass there."

"Perhaps." He smiled, and she was amazed at how his features softened as he did so. This man should smile more often, she thought. But Indians are not known to be smiling people. Remember who he is.

She climbed out of the canoe, her feet sinking into the marshy edge. Duval dismounted, threw their packs onto high and dry ground, picked up their canoe and placed it in the crotch of a nearby tree.

"I will build a fire, catch a fish if I can find one. You will collect wood, enough to last until dark. We will eat when I return. You are under protection here, so be not afraid while I am gone."

"Whose protection?"

"Little Bear's. His scouts will defend you if you need it."

They were being watched! Had the scouts seen her bathing? Did they watch as he had kissed and caressed her?

He laughed—an astonishing sound, rusty and creaking, as though he had not done much laughing, or very often. "They do not watch the object of protection, *Mademoiselle*. They patrol the area around the person."

He had read her mind. Did he also see the turmoil there, the tension in her body? If so, he gave no indication of it, but removed a hook and a length of twine from his pack, and a bag of meal that he dumped out onto a broad leaf. Stuffing the twine into the bag, threading the hook into the material at its mouth, he disappeared the way they had come.

What would happen tonight? Would he apply his seductive wiles on her? Or would he simply over-power her and take what he wanted. Should she try to resist? Where would she sleep?

Picking up small dry twigs, then larger ones, she made a pile. Then small dead branches that they could lay on top and feed in as the fire required, as she had seen them do when they camped on *Île St. Jean*. Her thoughts churned endlessly as she found more and more branches and tinder, fueled by a certain excitement, anticipation—yes, eagerness, even—whenever she allowed herself to remember his lips on hers, lightly seeking, teasing, taking. Within was a writhing, deep down, whenever she relived the memory of his mouth on her breasts, her throat, her own mouth . . .

Stop! She commanded. She had collected enough wood—and now?

Recalling that Madame Carrerot had given her a second set of clothing, she rummaged through her pack and found the short gown, shook it out. It would be good for sleeping, she thought, but the ground would be hard and there was no Armand to soften it with fir tips.

She could hear him coming, now, making noise so she was forewarned. The bag was full of frogs, not fish, all of them decapitated and gutted.

"These will keep us until morning," he explained, without praising her for the wood gathering she had done. He peeled some birch bark from one of the logs. Some fluffy stuff he'd gathered during his sojourn to the frog-catching place. A few dry, crispy leaves. Showered the little pile with sparks from his flints. A tiny thread of smoke appeared. "We'll take the cornmeal I've poured onto that leaf, mix it with a little water—" from his pack he removed a small flat stone with a shallow indentation in the middle—"lay it on the coals. Cook it until it's soft."

"And here I thought squaws did all the cooking."

"When the village is together, that is so. But a man in the middle of the wilderness needs to feed himself, so the women teach us how."

The frogs were not bad, all things considered, their bones soft and chewable, their flesh tender and crisp.

"Tell me where we are going," she said as they ate. "About Fort Lawrence. How does it come to be in the middle of nowhere."

"The French have built forts in strategic places to ensure supplies can reach Quebec and Louisbourg by land. One of these lies ahead. It is called Beausejour. The British have built their own fort nearby, to neutralize it. That is Fort Lawrence, and it is only by the greatest of bad luck that Paul-Henri was caught stealing supplies from its garrison. But he has always been a daring fellow."

"And, perhaps, stupid?"

"That depends on how badly you need the supplies."

The cornmeal, now cooked to mush, was gritty and supremely unsatisfying, but she gulped it down with large swallows of water. The meal would stick to her ribs; the frogs would not.

And then it was time. The woods began to gather darkness, the last glimmers of sun touching only the tree tops now.

"Have you prepared a satisfactory place for your sleeping robe?" he asked blandly, unfurling his own. "No? Well, then, spread it opposite mine, with the fire between us. I will keep it going through the night, so that you will be not alarmed in the dark should you rouse."

"Thank you," she choked, and spread her robe, checking for stones and sticks. There were none, but the ground was uncomfortable none the less, perhaps not as hard as the floor of last night's tipi, certainly not as hard as the galley of the schooner, but her body, unaccustomed to anything but a bed, set up protest. Her hips ached no matter how she lay. The pack with Madam Carrorot's extra clothing formed a reasonable pillow, the short gown remaining inside it, for she could not divest herself of her Indian clothes in Duval's presence. And then there was his unaccountable behavior, so blank and so correct, as though their encounter by the pool never happened. It filled her mind as she shifted from one side to another throughout the short night, miserable, confused, frustratated. The dark shadow across the fire never moved . . . and then it was morning.

    They walked.
    And walked.
    And walked.
    He considerately set a slow pace, held branches back so that she could pass easily, was never out of sight, waiting until she caught up. At noon they stopped for water and pemmican.
    "I'm sorry to say my feet are getting sore," she told him. "I will take your pack. Perhaps less weight on them will help."
    On they struggled—or, at least, she struggled—until, at what must have been mid-afternoon, he told her he must speak to a scout, that she should follow the path as best she could and he would come back for her soon. He moved ahead, further and further, and then disappeared.
    The wilderness closed in around her. The brambles and low hanging branches reached for her without Duval there to subdue them; gamely she forced herself on. After all, she had no pack! She had no excuse. She must try. Winning his respect somehow seemed very important—but the moccasins rubbed; the leggings were hot, the breech-clout chafed.
    Despite her determination to appear calm and in control of herself, she began to cry, silent tears running down her face, dripping onto her new tunic. She was unable to control them; she was churning inside, a welter of merciless thoughts creating turmoil, her sore feet more than an inconvenience. They had become a source of real pain.
    She stopped. Flying insects whizzed by; those in the brush sang into the silence, and as she listened, she heard water trickling, trickling slowly. Leaving the path, she limped toward the

sound, and found a rivulet, meandering placidly through the woods. Kneeling by it, she drank, bathed her face. Limping back to the path, she dragged a fallen branch across the trail, pointing toward the tiny brook. Duval would come back, no doubt. With the help of the branch he would find her—and then?

Ah, Mademoiselle, I see you have requested my presence. Perhaps to continue where we left off?

She would deny it. She would berate him for leaving her behind. For abandoning her when her feet were so sore and she was so hot and . . . her tears began again.

Stop this! She demanded of herself, and slipped off the moccasins and lowered her feet into the blessed coolness. Relief rippled head to toe through her. Distantly a bird sang.

His approach was again silent. He said nothing as he sat down.

"You found me, I see."

"Yes. It was good thinking, to leave a branch marking your place."

"I am becoming a woods-woman. And if you think I'm going to tell you how sorry I am that I stopped, you are wrong."

"I know," he said.

She glanced at him to see if he were as calm as he sounded. After all, there was a deadline to meet, was there not? But he seemed unconcerned. He poked at the bottom of the brooklet with a stick, stirring up small whirls of silt that settled back a few paces downstream.

"But, of course, I am delaying you," she ventured.

"Yes." More poking. Finally he looked up at her. "Do your feet hurt you?"

"Yes. And unlike your Indian women-folk, I do not sing. Instead, I complain."

"Why don't you try?"

"I am. I am complaining. Right this moment."

"Try singing."

"Surely you jest."

"Try."

Exasperated, she took a deep breath to steady herself, let it go, and sang.

Watching her closely, he said, "I didn't know you had such a voice."

"You never asked," she laughed.

"And your feet? How are they now?"

In fact she had forgotten they were sore.

"It is as I thought. But they need rest. We must stay a while."

Oh, Lord, oh God, guard me, she thought. While it looked like gallantry—his coming back, sitting down with her, making sure no harm came to her, protecting her—she was quite sure none of these were in his mind just now.

"I have made a camp up ahead, and have left our packs there. I will snare a bird for supper," he went on. "Or a rabbit. There is a low sweeping hemlock there that will shelter you as you sleep. It is very thick, and will protect you from the morning dew."

"And you?" she asked. There was no mistaking his intent.

"It is not the way of the People to force an encounter, *Mademoiselle*. A man is not obliged to accept the invitation of a woman, and our women have the final decision, whether or not to know a man. If I have mistaken your message, I will find a separate tree under which to sleep."

Confused as a maiden being courted for the first time, she found herself saying, "It would be easier if you simply seduced me, *Monsieur*."

Had she really said such a thing?

He laughed. "So that you take no responsibility, is that not so?"

The heat flooding her face made thinking more difficult. "I c,can't just—just agree," she stammered. "It would be un,unmaidenly."

"I think you mean, unPuritan."

"We are not Puritans. But by any standard, I would be considered wanton if I said I wished to lie with you."

"So you would like me to force you. Very well. I shall help," Gently he turned her face to his; the kiss conveyed warmth and affection and admiration, and then it became deeper, more intimate, and she pulled away only with enormous effort.

"What about the g,garrison? At Fort Lawrence? How f,far away is it? Do the English soldiers r,remain behind the walls of their fort all day, and all n,night? Will any of them be scouting about? Are the Mi'kmaq scouts watching?"

"The soldiers are terrified of the natives. If they go outside the fort itself, they go en masse, protecting each other with much noise and firings of their guns. If any of them march in our direction, the scouts will warn us, and we will hide. Now, then, I will show you the hemlock."

He gathered her up and carried her back to the path and to the site he'd selected, not so very far away. In fact, within calling distance. If she'd needed help, he would have heard her voice. A huge hemlock overlooked a clearing where he had set stones for a fire, with a small pile of kindling beside it.

"There. *Nous sommes arrivé.*"

Gently he placed her on her feet. "Your heart beats heavily," he murmured. "I can see it." He laid a light finger on the throbbing pulse in her throat. Close, so closely, they stood there, looking into one another's eyes. "If you are agreeable, we shall make a fire and I shall catch a rabbit. We shall eat. I have made you a bed of moss and pine tips beneath the great tree, over there—" He gestured toward the hemlock where, indeed, his robe was spread—"Upon it we will lie together. I will cover you with my body, if you permit. And tomorrow I will show you how to become one with the little stream back there, where I found you, and listen to the sounds of the woods and hear the songs of the earth, as the Great One intended."

He smiled, his eyes feasting on the fineness of her skin, the hollow of her throat. His mouth was tender, his lips soft against the softness of her mouth. He kissed her slowly, without hurrying, as though waiting for her to meet him in a secret place.

He stepped back, watching her with the sureness of a man who knew how to satisfy a woman. "I like you in your new clothes, but you would be better without them."

She looked down at herself, her garments.

In for a pence, in for a pound, she thought, and recklessly pulled the sleeveless shirt over her head while he watched.

She felt herself growing very warm. "Did you get these clothes from Red Bird?" she asked, trying to seem worldly and at ease.

"Forget Red Bird." Then he laughed. "But of course! You believe her performance on the river bank was a way to remind me of the evening we had just spent."

"Wasn't it?"

"She wanted me to remember occasions that we have shared in the past—but contrary to appearance, she was not reminding me of the hours recent, for I did not lie with her. I thought of you, and slept in the hut of unmarried men." He reached for one of the leggin strings, tied to the breech clout strap around her waist.

"We have a few days," he said as he fussed with it. "In them I will teach you to enjoy the wilderness. We will walk only short distances. If necessary, I will carry you on my back. There is much to learn, if you are willing, and at night we can watch the stars between the branches of the trees. But I will ask once more; I will not ask again. Am I repugnant to you?"

Barely able to breathe for the coursing of blood in her veins, she no longer heard birds in the trees or squirrels and the distant stream trickling, and helplessness overtook her—warm, pervasive. "You are far from repugnant, Marc Duval," she breathed. "And you know it."

His hand was firm on her breast, caressing it, and they were instantly back in that morning's moment, their blood still boiling.

"Shall I stop?" he murmured. "I think you are well ready for loving. I can feel your heat—but I can still stop, if you wish it."

"Please don't," she whispered, caught in a tide running so strong she could not hold it back. All the restraint she had ever known slipped forever out of reach. "Don't stop." She pressed against him while within grew an agonized need which only he could appease. He carried her to the hemlock and, lowering her upon his sleeping robe, he lay beside her, his lips warm on her closed eyes, and on her face and throat, her breasts and the hollow of her stomach as he untied her breech clout.

Then he tore off his own clothing and swung over her, his knees wedging her legs apart.

"Will anyone see?" she whispered, yearning, aching with the intensity of her need for him.

"No one." He spread her woman-place wide and prepared himself to enter, then pushed.

Now nearly breathless as something deep leaped and carried her along, she cried out and he stopped.

"I am hurting you."

Yes, it did hurt—it hurt very much—but she was so intent, so ready, that the pain was only on the edges of her awareness as she whispered, "Please, please, finish what you have begun."

Duval looked down at her, his arms straight so as to take his weight from her, his heavily muscled shoulders knotted and quivering, his eyes hot as iron on the anvil. He pushed a little deeper, waited carefully, thrust deeper. "Is it well?"

"Yes!" she whispered. "It is well."

He withdrew and then carefully thrust more deeply. "And now?"

"It is well!" she cried, caught up in her rising exaltation and her overwhelming need that opened to him, deep and terrible, obliterating the pain of her deflowering. Then he shuddered, quickly withdrew, rolled away. He was quiet, covered with sweat, and she waited for him to look at her, to speak, to return from wherever it was he had gone.

He shifted to his side to look at her. "You do look very beautiful just now." His eyes praised her, and all that she was and ever would be was his.

"Soon, if you are agreeable, I shall catch a rabbit while you collect more wood for the fire. We shall eat, and when it is dark we shall lie together again. This time I shall be able to wait, during our embrace, for as long as it takes you to have satisfaction. The first time with any man is rarely good for the woman. The second is much better. You shall see."

"And you have known many women," she teased.

"I have never deceived anyone about that, and I do not deceive you. I am in adoration of women. I always have been."

"You're a hard man, Marc Duval. You are supposed to lie, so that I will feel better."

"There are many ways to make you feel better." He ran a hand from her hip to her breast, kissed the pink nipple and laughed when it instantly tightened.

"By tonight you will be well ready," he said softly. She was ready now, and he knew it. He laughed again, and with his hand teased. "Tonight. You will be glad we waited. You will have less pain, and ecstasy belongs to starlight. We will move on to the

English fort from here, but slowly and I will show you the ways of the earth and the sky and the woods and you shall be my own Singing Bird, wild and free."

"And then we part, you and I. Forever."

"Think not of that. Think of this day, this moment. Let us not waste it! Let us take it, use it, live for it alone in the time that is given us by the Great One. Let me show you, Marguerite! Let me!"

The tight planes of his face were soft with tenderness and desire.

"Yes," she smiled. Oh, yes! "Show me how to use the time we have."

She relinquished the day, the hour, the moment. A part of her inner self unfurled to meet him, a part of herself that she could not contain, could not control nor wanted to—a part of herself more real, more true than she had known she possessed. She would learn what it meant to love a man for the instant given, for an hour, for a night, for as long as they had, to dwell in the eternal moment.

Maybe this is why captives go native, she thought as she looked up through the branches of a newly leafed tree—she did not know what kind of tree it was. Each morning, when she awakened, there was a new tree sheltering them, a new sky, a new world created for just the day ahead.

The river was far behind now, but there were many springs to stop beside, take a meal, or set up camp as they made their way to Fort Lawrence. Duval seemed to know where roots could be dug up, cleaned up, nibbled upon. Ferns were sprouting and their tender tips were a pleasant accompaniment to the rabbits and squirrels that served as meals; along the trail they chewed endlessly on pemmican from his pack.

He was awake already, watching her as she came up out of her dreams.

"Don't you ever sleep?" she had asked.

"While I am on the trail," he had answered, "not much. I am always on watch—for the safety of my men, or just now, you."

He always knew when she was awake, even before she opened her eyes. How?

"Mi'kmaqs believe there are two souls within us—a spirit one, and a body one. In sleep, the spirit soul departs, to speak to the spirits of ancestors and animals. When it returns, or when it is needed, it enters your body again and you are whole. My spirit soul knows when yours becomes present."

"If I woke before you, would I know when your soul returned?"

"Your spirit soul would, but you are not yet attuned to these things. You are white. White people are notoriously bad at such understanding. But I like your white body." He began to kiss it, and then kissed more, and licked and nibbled and again took her up, worked her into a frenzy.

Spineless, without any strength at all, she cried—"Now! Now!"

For in the middle of it all, she understood. Within the sexual embrace, at least, she knew how two people became one person, completely wrapping one another up in tendrils of exquisite ecstasy that hovered near, but never actually touched, pain's domain. And then, released to fly free, to merge with the heartbeat of the earth, to lose oneself there, come back to the spirit soul of the beloved . . . .

You are becoming a pagan already, Margaret Roberge, she told herself.

It was true.

And it was good.

CHAPTER

8

Fort Lawrence

The woods thinned out the further north they travelled, and stumps appeared. Many of them. "For fuel," he told her. "Acadians no longer farm the land here, but some have set up camp temporarily to supply the fort with wood; some live across that little river, yonder, where is the French Fort Beausejour, and bring wood to it also. There used to be a settlement here, called Beaubasson," he went on. "The priest LeLoutre wanted the Acadians to move down to Grand Pré so everyone would be close together, and once they went, he burned their houses down so they could not return."

"We have a saying," she told him. "It goes: 'With friends like that, who needs enemies?'"

"The priest thought he was helping. There is more at stake here than a farm or a herd of cattle. A way of life is threatened. Just as it is with your kind, in Boston."

"The Huguenots?"

"Yes. You told me your church had closed. Soon none of you will be speaking French. You won't even remember that you are French. The same applies to Acadia. The English will move in, build a church, and only members will have a say in how the community functions."

"It was like that at the beginning of our colony. But not now."

"It will be just like that until Acadian ways have died out. How long do you think your family will be speaking French?"

"As long as we are in trade. My father is not a clerk, although I told you he was."

"You must have thought it seemed more harmless?"

"Yes," she chuckled. "He owns a company that has been in Roberge hands for many years. We import damask from Ireland, where the Huguenots set up mills. One day we may trade with France again, import wines and laces along with the Irish linen. One day I will be the owner of my father's company and I will speak French, and my children will speak it, too."

Duval was lying on his back, looking at the sky as he listened. "I am amazed, dear Marguerite. Your father grooms you for a man's job?"

"He has no other heir, and wants to keep the business in the family."

"Our women can be chiefs, did you know?"

"A lady chief?" She tried to picture a scrawny, elderly squaw with a feathered war bonnet on her greasy old hair, tomahawk and axe belted at her bony hip.

"Sometimes women must carry the burdens of men. Just as your father wants you to do."

"And I am glad he does. It makes life more interesting than just waiting for the right man to show up and marry me and take all my rights away." For the first time in many days, she thought of Robert Blake. It was as though a shadow fell across her, and she shivered.

"What is it?" he asked.

"I am to be married to a man I do not love."

"I thought the English did not marry for the sake of love."

"It is not a requirement. But now, having been loved by you, it will be much harder."

"Have you never loved one of your own kind?"

"I have." She told him about Tyler Moore, about the Colonial Press, about the plan to print Samual Adams' writings with the money she could get from Roberge Imports, once she was in charge.

"I have heard about this man Adams. He understands duplicity of the English and tries to make others also understand. Is that not so?"

"Yes." She took his hand. "Marc, why do you hate the English so much? I know they are enemies of France, but your hatred is much deeper than politics. This I know."

"These English will kill every Indian they can find, whose birthright this land is."

He spat into the fire to prove his contempt.

"There is more to your hatred than you are telling me." She kept her voice quiet, low, but firm. "I think your hatred of the English is personal, Marc. I think they have injured you in some very real and deep way. I would know what it is they have done."

He stared into the sky for a long time, then looked over at her. "My mother was Malacite, a people who lived between the ocean and the mountains. The English call it Maine. Some years ago the English built a fort on the great river Kennebec, to protect the white settlers who were colonizing there. It became a trading post, as many forts did, and was a gathering place for the local population as well as the British soldiers when they were off duty.

"I do not know that it was an English soldier who raped my mother. I only believe it. English always just take what they want. I think he caught her gathering raspberries, for they were in season—they always are, in August. And our women always do the berry picking."

He was getting wrapped up in irrelevant details, but she was careful not to hurry him or indicate impatience. He must come to it in his own way.

"Whoever it was, he raped her and then went away. My mother's family adopted me—Indians do this easily. They treasure children. Little boys and girls are their future, full blooded or not. They can learn tribal secrets and ensure rest for the departed. I was raised for ten summers by the Malacite and would have become one with them had not the English soldiers come back. They butchered everyone they could find and burned the huts and threw the dead onto the flames.

"I was not there when the massacre happened. I had gone into the woods to find a place where I could stay when my time came to prove myself a man. This proving—it starts early for us, and part of it is remaining alone for a time, in the place already chosen. When I came back there was nothing left. I hid in the woods until the ashes were cold. I dug a hole in a secret place and buried as much of them as I could. The Malacite, and I am sure most Indians, believe that the following generations must place grave goods where the spirit soul of the dead can find them and be at peace. A ceremony establishing the village grave site can be performed later when the People defeat the English. They are there waiting. My mother, my family, my friends."

No wonder he was so intent on Acadia taking Maine back!

"Some *coureurs du bois* found me wandering in the woods. They fed me, took me in their canoes to a French post on the St. Lawrence. The post had a mission—Jesuit—to convert the Indians. They took me in, fed and clothed me, taught me French, Latin and English, made me into a Catholic so that I would become a missionary, like them. But of course I could not be a priest, because I am partly Indian. I am not good enough, in the eyes of the church. So I decided that if I was not good enough to become a priest, I was not good enough to be a missionary, either. When I was fourteen I ran away and found Little Bear, whom you know. He is as a father to me, his tribe adopted me, and they hate the British as much as I do. I believe our hatred is well placed. That is why I was so rude to you when first we met and I believed you were English, too."

"And now you know I am American. Am I correct?"

"Yes, yes." His tone was somewhat less than enthusiastic.

"The wealthy among us pretend to be British, and they hope to return to England in a much higher estate than their forebears. But most people in the colonies—the common people—consider themselves American. It is not the same thing."

He shook his head. "You must do as the English tell you—like it or not. They use you, and you let them."

"And the French are better?"

"They do not kill natives. They share the land we apportion to them. They do not try to take for themselves something that no one can own. The land is a gift, just as game is a gift. They take no more than they need. But the English would take it all."

Indeed they would, she knew. That was why everyone had come to the New World, was it not? For land? That was the American dream . . . .

※

The next morning, spirals of smoke appeared on the horizon.

"It is nearly time to part," Duval said, without inflection. "Put on the clothes Madame Carrerot gave you."

Unable to move, she simply stood there, watching the smoke.

His face softened. "It is over, my dearest Singing Bird. It is over. See? The huts of the Acadians are yonder. Please, Marguerite. Change your clothes, now. Do not make this harder than it already is."

The Acadian dwellings were rough, no more than bark go-downs, obviously temporary. Most of the men were gone, foraging for fuel further away. The women were left behind to cook dinner over open fires, both for their men and for the English garrison at Fort Lawrence.

"*Bonjour*, Marc!" they called. "We've been expecting you!"

"If you've been expecting me, then Armand St. Martin must be here already."

In fact, he was approaching from the far end of the enclave. "Where in the name of *le bon Dieu* have you been?"

"Have you arranged for the exchange?" Marc temporized.

Armand looked at them closely. "Shall I assume that you both had a pleasant week? I think you have timed everything well, Marc. I have been negotiating, as you instructed me to do, and I have received word that the Grand Pré raiders have made it to *La Riviere St. Jean*. If you hurry, perhaps we—you and Paul-Henri and I will be in time."

"*Bien*."

"The English are expecting a girl in women's clothing. Madam LeFebvre has vacated her place for the, er, hostage to use. We'll go to the fort as soon as she can be made ready. Paul-Henri waits there. Come, I will tell you everything while *Mademoiselle* Robinson changes her clothes. Bonsoleil is in charge. The man is a genius. We'll all dress as Indians, put on war paint, and no one will know who is Acadian and who is not . . ."

Marc and Armand turned away and a woman plucked at Margaret's sleeve. "*Suivez-moi*. Follow me."

You will lose him now, she told herself. But she understood that she had never possessed him, that their arrival here meant they most likely would not speak intimately again.

The LeFebvre shanty was much like the ones on the shores of Louisbourg. A wattle and daub fireplace filled one end, with a rough table and chairs in the middle of the place, blankets folded in a pile at the back. At the entrance a length of loose-woven material let in some light.

On the low table lay a mug, some bread and cheese and a pitcher of water. Draped over a rustic chair was a chemise with sleeves sewn onto it, and an enormous kerchief to fold over the shoulders and bosom, a patched petticoat and an apron. There were no shoes, nor a cap.

The LeFebvre woman fetched a bowl and a small cloth for washing, set them on the table beside the pitcher. Taking a comb from the pocket in her apron, she laid it beside the bowl and pointed to Margaret's shorn hair, getting a bit longer now, and able to be neatened up. Looking her critically up and down, she shrugged and left, pushing through the entrance curtain.

She thinks I am English, Margaret thought. She doesn't know we could speak together. And yet, what is there to say?

The water was tepid. She scrubbed her face with the cloth provided, rinsed the rest of her body as best she could and struggled into the finery provided for her. How strange a skirt felt! She flung the kerchief around her shoulders, securing it with the petticoat and apron strings, put the garments Marc had given her into her pack, as well as the clothing provided by Madame Carrerot and sat down on a stool to wait.

She had left her moccasins on. How clumsy they felt with a skirt clinging to them.

But this was the least of her worries.

Marc.

How could she just leave him?

Put him behind her, a memory...

Time had no meaning, those brief days in the wilderness, flowing as a languid, sensual dream, in which she had learned—all too well—what it meant to be free. And what it meant to love. Now—now they had run out of time.

He was totally absorbed in leading his men, his Acadians, his Mi'kmaqs. It hurt, knowing that his private, personal Singing Bird was so easily put aside—though he had never promised anything else. This she knew. This she had always known.

The curtain was pushed aside and he slipped in. "Are you here, *ma petite*? It is dark. I cannot see! Where are you?"

She moved swiftly to him, slid into his arms, pressed as close as she could. Beneath her ear she could hear the even, steady pulsing of his heart. "Ah. Here you are," he murmured into her hair.

She must speak with him now or lose the chance.

"Tell me what will happen," she whispered, her lips brushing the smooth skin at the base of this throat.

"Paul-Henri and Armand and I will go to the river Saint John. If Bonsoleil has not attacked already, we will join him and surround the warship in canoes at night. There is a cannon in the fort. It will fire upon the British ship, and will be our signal to throw grappling hooks over the edge and swarm up, take them from behind as they attend to the fort."

"It sounds dangerous."

"It has worked before. Last year we took several British schooners that way."

"They are much smaller than a British warship."

Eyes accustomed to the dimness now, he held her from him with admiration. "You know the difference?"

"Of course. I am from Boston. We make our living on the sea and ships." This was not what she wanted to talk about. "Marc, please—"

"It matters not if you tell the English about this. Or even about the fleet. By the time they understand, it will be too late for them." He ran his fingers through her hair. "Our time draws short, Marguerite. I—I know not what to say."

"Just kiss me," she begged, her voice unsteady. "Now. Right now."

His lips were urgent, even frantic—a side of him she had never seen, he who was always so self-possessed, in control. She met his embrace, was lost in it. They clutched at one another, their blood and torment rising.

"Oh, God!" he whispered. "How can it be? How can it be?"

"Marc, send me over to Fort Beausejour," she wept, "and from there to Quebec City. Please! Find another English person to exchange."

A muffled sound came from deep in his throat. "It will not work, Little Bird," he said brokenly. "There is no other person to exchange. And Beausejour is not well defended. There may be no one there who could take you to Quebec."

"Then let me wait here until you come back. I can talk with these people. I can stay with them until you can come to me."

He smoothed her hair, kissed her throat. "I do not believe the Acadians here would welcome you in their midst, if you were to stay. They are more puritan than the *Bostonais*, and they are not stupid. They know how we have spent this week, and why I was late in arriving."

He wiped away a tear that escaped down her cheek. "You are a lovely woman, Mar-gar-et," he said softly, emphasizing the English pronunciation of her name. "So lovely." He stepped back, then, and faced her squarely. "Acadia will be at war soon, and all of

New France. Quebec City will be under fire, surely as Beausejour and Louisbourg. There will be no safe place for you—only will there be safety in the American colonies. You must continue as planned. To Boston. To your father. To your beloved. To your betrothal, if you must. The exchange—you for Paul-Henri, must go forward." He looked deeply into her eyes, as though to take a part of her with him. "And through the exchange, you will be protected by the British army if war should come before you can get out."

"I will be gone from your life, forever."

They could hear a woman's voice rising, another arguing with her, another hushing them.

"Yes," he said, his voice now quiet and firm.

There was a commotion outside. "Marc!" Armand called.

He did not answer. His eyes were haunted. Was he rent asunder, as she was? Did he hurt? Did he ache? Did he wish to scream at the sky and protest his fate? Her throat was dry, her heart beat in her ears like distant thunder.

"I am a man with a mission," he said finally. "I know who my enemies are. I will not—I cannot rest—until they are vanquished, or my people are."

She asked, her voice trembling, "And if you are defeated, Mark—or even if they are—what then?"

He did not answer. There was no answer possible.

Stunned and empty, she could think of nothing more to say. She could no longer prevent the slide into despair. For she could not hold him.

He looked for a last, desperate moment into her eyes, waiting as though a magic turn of events would save them from this moment, undo it, and replace it with kindness and love. As though to gather strength.

CHAPTER EIGHT

Then he turned from her and held back the cloth. He gestured her through, his face blank now, as though she were a visiting lady. Waited.

Slowly, slowly, her strength returned, and her pride. A dalliance, was it, with a few sweet words, a night or two of passion? All right! She could accept that, because she must.

She walked past him as though she had never seen him before, into the blinding daylight with her head high and her back straight.

Armand waited.

"Ah, *Monsieur* St. Martin," she said lightly, loudly enough to be heard by the occupant of the little hut, still standing in the doorway, watching. "My dear Armand, it is so delightful to see you again."

"Indeed it is a delight, *Mademoiselle*. Allow me to take your pack."

"Oh, yes," she simpered. "Thank you."

"Soon you will be home, *Mademoiselle!*"

"Indeed, I will," she trilled, and, trailed by her broken hopes, her aching heart, she left him. To his destiny, to his people, to his mission.

She did not look back to see if he were watching, because she was afraid he was not. She only walked on, listening to Armand, and wondered when she would become mercifully numb.

CHAPTER

9

The Refugee

She could see Papa waiting at the base of Long Wharf as the packet from Halifax settled into its appointed place.

Beside him was Robert Blake, waving his hat. Behind them both was the Blake coach, its driver and two men in livery.

Yes, she was home, the endless journey done. The gangplank was run out and secured; the captain appeared, witness to safe delivery of the hostage.

"Good luck to you, Mistress."

It had taken only a day, from Halifax to Boston, the weather and wind perfect. She'd sat in the aftercabin, hands primly folded, watching without noticing as the Atlantic passed by.

"Allow me to escort you so there's no danger you'll fall into the harbor," the captain offered, once the ship was secured.

"Thank you." Her smile was wooden as she took his arm, but it was the best she could do.

"Those gentlemen at the far end of the wharf—are they here to meet you?"

"Yes."

"I shall take you to them."

But it was unnecessary. Robert, having left Papa, was already drawing near. She curtseyed to the captain and turned in Robert's direction, her pack clutched tightly to her chest, hand outstretched to forestall his embrace. Her pack, all she had of Marc, stuffed with her sleeping robe and Indian apparel and Armand's blue blanket.

"Margaret! Dear Margaret!" He kissed her hand and then held it captive in both of his. "We were told you were alive and safe. The commander of Fort Lawrence wrote us. We've been waiting with bated breath, as it were."

Winslow had sent word! "How?" she asked. Robert seemed not to understand. "How was Major Winslow able to get word to you so soon?"

It was not a question that Robert expected.

"I'm not sure, my dear. I'll find out, if it is important to you."

"Thank you. It is."

He tucked her hand under his arm, and they began to walk. "About your father . . ."

Of course, she must bring her attention to the present moment. Papa was still waiting at the far end of the wharf, with the Blake servants.

"Your dear father is not himself. When we heard about the *Lady Nan*, he seemed to just—just disintegrate."

No buffoonery was present in Robert's voice, nor superior smugness. He seemed truly concerned. Disintegrate!

"What do you mean?"

"He took to his bed, and he didn't leave it. You realize, of course, that we did not know you had been found and rescued. All of us believed we had lost you both."

"I must go to him, Robert."

Freeing herself, she ran.

"Meg! My precious Meg!" Into his outstretched arms she threw herself, his tears of joy mingling with hers. "I can hardly believe it." His voice was that of an old man, warbling. "I can hardly believe it!"

His legs were shaking. Indeed, his whole body shook. "I can hardly believe it," he said again, and began to cry.

Robert had caught up. "Sir, let us get into the coach."

Papa's tears stopped. The two footmen approached at Robert's signal, clasped wrists in a fireman's carry and bent low. Perching on the seat they created, Papa was carried like a king to the coach and helped in.

"How long has he been this way?" Margaret asked as she and Robert watched.

"As I told you. When he heard the ship had foundered and everyone believed both you and your dear mother had perished. The shock of it was more than he could bear."

"He had a slight stroke last winter . . ." she remembered. "It sounds as though he's had another." Oh, Papa!

Robert helped her into the coach. "My family and I are so sorry, both about your mother and also about your father. He is as good as lost also, I'm afraid."

Lost. Papa was lost. Mama was lost.

As she looked around at the Boston waterfront and its markets and wharves, its surrounding hills and a myriad chimneys smoking thinly into the warm sky, Mama's death became real again. The last time she'd been here, Mama so excited, Papa so determined to make sure his only child would be ready to run his business, their future awaiting . . . .

Sitting next to her father, she covered his folded hands with her own. "I am so happy to see you," she whispered in his ear, and kissed his cheek. Robert climbed in; the coachmen handed him a shawl to spread over Papa's frail knees, and the coach moved off.

"I can hardly . . . ," Papa stopped short of repeating himself. "My precious Meg, what has happened to your hair?"

"A good question," Robert cried jovially. "Looks like she was lucky not to be scalped."

"My travels through Acadia required my passing as a boy," she told them. To her chagrin, the tears she had been able to hold at bay rose up now from the deep well of grieving that was a permanent part of her now. They poured down her face. Robert's unctuous smile instantly fell away.

"Oh, my dear!" He slid from his seat and knelt on the coach floor in front of her, his hands over hers and Papa's. "Forgive me! I'm so sorry! I should have realized how overwrought you must be! I'm so sorry, dear Margaret!"

Papa freed a hand from the pile on his lap and patted her shoulder, crooning, "Meg. Our Meggie. Meggie has come home."

It was too much, too much. She'd been held at Fort Lawrence under the most primitive of conditions until the prisoner Paul-Henry was delivered to Marc—somewhere in the fort. The commander was too busy to talk. He dispatched a sedan chair to the Bay of Fundy. A small sailing vessel carried her across the Minas Basin, over to a river. After countless portages and carries, she arrived in Halifax. In the harbor, the French ship caught at the Saint John River rode at anchor. Obviously Bonsoleil's plan had failed. Where was Marc now?

The carriage stopped. One of Blake's men dismounted, opened the door and there, at the foot of the portable steps, was Lucy.

Sliding into the coachman's arms, then into Lucy's, Margaret held her dear cousin close. "Get rid of him," she wept. "Robert. Make him go away."

"It's our Meg!" It was Cook, who embraced her from behind even as Lucy held her from the front.

The footman helped Papa down; Robert followed.

"I suppose this display is only to be expected of someone who has been through what she has been through," he said to Lucy, trying to find something of Margaret he could touch—her arm, her cheek—"weeping and carrying on and all."

"I believe you're right. I hope you will accept our apologies, Mr. Blake," Lucy simpered. "I think I'd better get her to bed."

"Of course!" Robert agreed as he climbed back into the coach. "It is only to be expected of so young and frail a flower. I only wish, ma'am, that there was something I could do. I'll call in the morning."

"That would be nice," Papa said. By now he, too, was part of the circle protecting Margaret. "We could play rummy, sir."

Papa never played cards.

Cook disengaged him. "Let's get some tea, Mr. Roberge."

"Will you play rummy with me?" Papa querried.

"I should love to!" Cook exclaimed, leading him toward the door as the coach pulled away.

"Come, my dearest Meg," Lucy sang softly. "You must rest. You'll feel better for it. Your room is ready."

"My pack. I had a pack," Margaret whimpered. "Where is it?"

"I have it," Cook called over her shoulder. "I'll bring it up later."

The house was cool and quiet.

"Here we go. Up the stairs." Lucy's strong arm swept her along.

Her chamber was exactly as she'd left it—canopied bed with curtains all around to keep her warm in winter, pinned up now in summer. Her little commode, a standing mirror to one side, her wardrobe on the other. Her expensive fashion doll on top, along with the summertime bonnets she'd gotten out of storage before she left. Chair in front of the window, candle stand by the head of her bed, hope chest at the foot.

"Your father used to come in here, and sit at the window, and just cry," Lucy told her. "He wanted to keep the chamber exactly as you left it. After a while he forgot why, but still he kept on sitting there, rocking back and forth."

"Robert said he was this way soon after he heard the *Lady Nan* went down."

"Yes, he was fine until then. It took the better part of two weeks for word of the shipwreck to reach us. The next day he refused to get out of bed. He didn't get up for a week, and wasn't himself when he did get on his feet again. That's when he started keeping vigil at the window." Lucy patted the quilts. "Please, darling Margaret, let me help you to get into bed. The news isn't good, and you'll must rest a while before we talk about it."

She let Lucy remove her dress and chemise, slipping a voluminous nightgown over her head. Easing herself into the softness of the pillows and the cradle of her down-filled mattress, every part of her body took its ease and she floated, weightless. It was relief of the highest order.

"Wait 'til you see what's in my pack," she whispered.

"I'll make sure it's here when you wake up," Lucy assured her. "We'll talk later. And you can tell me what happened to your hair." She grinned, teased one of the out-growing spikes, and stole away.

She must hide the pack somewhere! At the back of the wardrobe? Under her bed? Beneath the linens in her hope chest?

Hope.

Hope for what? Was there anything to hope for?

Don't think, she sleepily counseled herself. Don't . . . .

CHAPTER NINE

The setting sun crept over the city and suffused the little room as Lucy tip-toed in with a pot of tea and a slice of johnny cake.

"You're awake!" She pulled the chair up close to the head of the bed. "This is the third time I've brought this tray up. With fresh tea each time," she hastened to add. "Are you feeling more rested now?"

"Yes, thanks."

"Have you been awake long?"

"Long enough to figure out that everything has changed. Hold my hand and tell me what's really going on."

"You're sure you're up to it'"

"I'd better be," she said, and meant it. With Papa so limited, she must take charge.

"Oh! Before I forget, Robert's servant came by and left you this note." Lucy fetched it from her apron pocket.

"Fine, fine, thanks. Put it on the table." She poured herself a cup of tea and nibbled at the cake.

"Here's how everything happened. Uncle had a meeting with Robert's father just after you and your mother left. I'm quite sure they came to some kind of agreement, about a dowry and such. Then Uncle came down with a catarragh and stayed in bed a while; I ran the shop. He was getting better when came the news about the ship."

"Go on."

Lucy drew a deep preparatory breath. "Then, like I told you, he just stayed in bed, and soon it wasn't hard to see that he wasn't going to be able to run Roberge Imports. The Blakes helped for a while, and after a bit got guardianship so the company could continue, managed by them with our family expenses paid out of the profits. So Uncle can stay right here, with Cook and me to look after him—forever, I suppose."

"Lucy, it's the same as a merger!"

"Not legally. And if you were really dead, darling, it wouldn't matter."

"It would matter if you were to inherit Roberge. That was, I think, an idea Papa toyed with. If both Papa and I died . . ."

"Me!" Lucy scoffed.

"The business would stay in the family."

Lucy shook her head and poured herself a cup of tea.

"No matter." Margaret said briskly. "I am here, and guardianship isn't an issue."

"It might be. Your father clearly can't run the business, and you can't inherit it if he's alive. The Blakes will keep it going, and probably do a good job with it. Considering they expect you to marry Robert, ownership would pass to them eventually, in any case."

"Because of coverture."

"Yes."

"And I suppose it's too much to hope that Papa drew up the transfer to me before the *Lady Nan* went missing?"

"I haven't found anything on his desk."

"Well, I'm not married yet!" She threw the covers off. "I am in mourning. I can't think about marriage at this time. I don't understand why you and Papa aren't in black clothing already, and why he's not wearing an armband."

"Your father didn't want to go into mourning. It would require acceptance that your mother and you were dead."

"It's time he did accept it. Mama's d,death."

"Very well, I'll see to it. Next on the agenda is Tyler Moore."

Tyler! Tears welled up at the thought of him, and the effort it would take to deal with this complication. Pacing around the little room, Margaret came to rest at the open window. The gentle evening was settling in. Below, the tiny back garden and the gardens of their neighbors were hidden by the trees now in full leaf. When she and Mama had left, the foliage was still in bud. In a few months the Red Leaf Moon would rise, and the trees on the Pemberton Hill and Beacon Hill would erupt into masses of color, oranges and reds and golds, and the leaves of their own tree would fall and the room would be light again, and winter would start and somehow she would endure . . . a sob broke loose.

"I'm truly sorry!" Lucy exclaimed. "I don't mean to make you cry. Listen! There's good news to share. Master Wagner has died. He fainted while setting type for an advertisement. Tyler caught him and carried him into the house to Mistress Wagner, then went back and finished the printing job, ran up the invoice, delivered the job and collected the money due. The widow was very impressed and offered him his freedom in exchange for keeping the shop open until she can decide what to do. She pays him a decent wage and he can come and go as he pleases."

How quickly could one's fortune change!

"He's living over the shop, so he can look after the property by night as well as be nearby in case Mistress Wagner needs help. As soon as we heard you were coming home, I went to tell him. He said he wanted to see you, as soon as possible. He said that if you didn't agree, he would knock the door down and get to you by force." Margaret smiled weakly. Papa had forbidden Tyler to come to the house. A bound boy, calling on his daughter, was unthinkable for a merchant dealing in luxury imports.

"Of course I would like to see him," she said. "But as soon as I'm up and about, Robert will be in the parlor. And Madam Blake. And our family friends, and business associates, and church members—oh, God!"

"Wait! Hold on! You don't have to see anybody before you're ready, and certainly not tomorrow, when you've just arrived home. Tyler and I made a plan, and we can put it into action whenever you wish. Don't get upset, sweetheart."

"What's the plan?"

"He'll wait in the woodshed at midnight. I'll keep watch from the house, and you can go out to meet him. If anyone wakes up, I'll light a candle and you'll know to come back in, as though returning from the backhouse."

"It ought to work. Tomorrow night?"

"I'll arrange it. Meanwhile, you were going to show me what's in your pack." Lucy brought it out from the corner where she'd left it. Margaret scooted up to the headboard, Lucy sat at the foot; the pack was unstrapped and overturned.

Armand's blanket was on top.

"A very dear man gave this to me, to sit on when we had supper in the woods."

"You and he had supper?"

"Everyone had supper. We'd been on the river all day."

"In canoes, I suppose?"

"Yes. They were the only means of transport available." Of course, Lucy knew nothing about travelling in the wilderness. No one knew anything. Margaret might just as well have voyaged to the moon.

"So my friend gave me this blanket from one of the packs of trade goods—don't ask," she intercepted the next question. "When we have time, I tell you anything you'd like to know. But we slept out-of-doors every night, and this—" the fur robe was next –"this was mine to wrap up in."

Lucy fingered the tanned side. "It's very soft."

"And very comfortable, especially when you put stuff under it, like moss or grass."

"They gave you this?"

"They had to. Camping and canoeing was the only way to get me from Louisbourg to Fort Lawrence. I used it every night, so it became mine."

"Ah."

CHAPTER NINE

"And these were my clothes, to wear when we had to walk. It's called 'portage'. The canoes and the packs are carried . . ."

"Oh, gracious!" Lucy held up one leggin. Then the other. Found a moccasion. Then the breech clout.

"Can you explain this?"

"I can, but I'd rather do it later."

"Oh, surely! You must be getting tired. Inconsiderate of me, Meg. Are you hungry?" Lucy eyed the nibbled-upon johnny cake. "It doesn't look like it. Maybe breakfast will be more interesting. Suppose I leave you now. Your father will want to visit with you, and you and he can stay upstairs tomorrow while I explain to everyone that you need more time."

"Especially Robert."

"Yes. And don't forget the note he brought."

Ah, she had forgotten. No doubt a love ditty, since he must believe they were engaged.

Thou art fair indeed
Slender and graceful as a reed,
Lovely of feature, grace art thine
Even with hair like a porcupine!

Despite herself she laughed, and thought that perhaps he was not so bad, after all. His note was on the back.

'My dear, you asked about how the commander at Fort Lawrence notified Governor Shirley that you had been released. It seems that recently three gun boats and 21 transports were dispatched from Boston to the Bay of Fundy preparatory to taking a French fort nearby. Once the troops were off loaded, the transports returned with his message.

'I hope this satisfies your query. If there is more I can do, please do not hesitate . . . etc. etc. etc.'

Beausejour. The British/American forces had attacked Fort Beausejour by now. And if it had fallen—almost a certainty—the supply lines to Louisbourg and Quebec City were badly compromised and the British would have complete control. The Acadians easily could be deported from *Île St. Jean*, and once Louisbourg was starved out, the Acadians camped on *Île Royale* could be deported as well. Everything Marc was fighting for, and the Acadian leader Bonsoleil, and the priest LeLoutre, and the Mi'kmaqs too—everything was lost with the capture of Beausejour.

Their war is done, she told herself miserably. I can only hope the man I care about is somehow safe.

Now there is Tyler. I can fight for him.

But would he want her, once he learned about Marc?

Lucy led the way by the light of her candle. It was full dark, now, at midnight. The shed hulked ahead, then the doorway appeared in the candle's shadow. Then Tyler.

"Here she is!" Lucy hissed, then tactfully disappeared.

"Oh my God," Tyler breathed, not as an oath, but a prayer. "Oh, Meg!" He reached out, found her, embraced her, tight, tight, and she hugged him in return. Oh, it was so good to be back in his arms! "I thought you were dead, my darling." His voice quavered. "I thought you were dead, and then you came back and that damned Robert Blake brought you home. I didn't know what to do, where to turn, and then I remembered you telling me about your cousin Lucy—so I sent her a message..."

"I wish it had been you there to greet me, instead of Robert. Oh, Tyler, I must talk to you." She caressed his precious face. "I need you," she whispered.

"I need you, too." He brought her close again, sought her lips. But sensitive to her as he was, he detected resistance. "What is it, Margaret?" he asked softly.

Don't hide from him, she counseled herself. He sees into your soul. To deny the truth is to lose him, sooner rather than later.

"Oh, Tyler," she breathed, "I've been seized by pirates and imprisoned by the French and marched through the Acadian wilderness and stared at by Indians . . ." She took a breath.

Tell him now.

"A man named Marc Duval pulled me through most of it."

He was silent for a long time and then his arms fell away. "And you became enamored of him."

There was more to it than being enamored, but it was not a detail he wanted—or needed—to hear.

"Yes."

"And you love him still."

This is it.

"Yes."

He was silent for a long time. "Yet you have come to me. Willingly, so it seems."

"You are my first love, Tyler. You will always be. I have not changed toward you—not at all. But in the weeks I was gone, I became more than I was when I left. My love for you does not enter the new places of my heart, but it is as strong as ever in the old."

"And that is why you agreed to see me? To say you used to love me but now you love someone else?" he asked slowly.

"I didn't just 'agree' to see you. I wanted to be with you, my dearest friend." Oh, Tyler, she prayed. Do you love me enough? "Knowing Marc has not affected my sentiments toward you! He doesn't change the importance of your place in my life. I am in great need of your friendship."

He stepped away from her. "Knowing about this man changes things," he said finally. "He knows you as you are today, not as the maiden I loved in the back room of the print shop. Where is he now?"

"I don't know."

"So you've lost him, too. And now wish to resume relations with me, is that it?"

It was harsh, when looked at this way. But who could blame him?

"I would share with you the new maiden—woman—I have become."

"Why?"

"Because I believe you would understand her, once you learned her ways, her thoughts, her beliefs. Will you have her?"

A candle suddenly gleamed from the darkness of the house.

"I don't know. I have to give it time," he said. "Surely you can understand that."

"Yes, Tyler. Of course I do. I am asking much of you."

"Yes. You are."

"I must go. Lucy is signaling me. When can I see you again?"

"As I said, I need time," he said, his voice quite neutral. "I'll tell Lucy when—or if—I'm ready. Begone now."

He did not offer to kiss her again. He did not embrace her. He only stepped back, waiting for her to leave, and slowly she did, making her way to the light in the kitchen window.

CHAPTER

10

August

The Blake's mansion was a delight, impressively gilded and swathed in drapery and carpets as such a house in upper-class England would be. The family's pride in it was understandable, for it provided a gateway to their place in an eventual American aristocracy. The governor and his circle were entertained there. Visiting members of the nobility were invited to intimate dinner parties, and occasionally they accepted. Perhaps, one day, the king?

Their country estate in Medfield was another upward rung on the social ladder. Twice the Blakes had taken her and Papa there, sailing up the Mystic River with the tide and coming back to Boston on the ebb.

"Are there mystics living there?" Margaret had asked on her first tour. "Like hermits and sooth-sayers?" She'd grinned mischievously, so they would know she was jesting.

"Its name is 'Mis-i-tuk', the native word for 'high water'. Referring to its being a tidal river," Madam Blake lectured. "We always try to keep as close to the Indian names possible, so the natives will see we mean well."

"And refrain from scalping us in our sleep," Mr. Blake offered jovially.

"Pay him no attention, Miss Margaret," Robert intervened fondly.

A modest wharf jutted into the river at Medfield, where the family's little schooner docked when they visited. The house itself was a duplicate of the one in which they all were seated today in Boston, drinking tea and planning another trip, this one to lay out formal gardens in truly English style. Though labor for such work was not easy to find, Mr. Blake planned to rent some slaves from an upriver neighbor next spring, and the work would be accomplished quickly.

"Will you have more tea?" Robert's mother asked Papa. She was as impressively gilded and swathed as the parlor where they sat, in sharp contrast to the drab mourning worn by the Roberge father and daughter.

Drawing in her breath slowly, so no one would notice, Margaret glanced down at her folded hands, placidly lying on her lap, giving no hint of her trepidation. It was time to begin, and do it without alienating the Blakes. She needed their support for a while longer while she regained her ability to concentrate, act quickly and decisively if need be—and just now, she could not. She would most likely just curl up and cry in a crisis.

But the longer she delayed, the more entrenched was their position as guardians.

"No." Papa shook his head briskly. "A biscuit. I want a biscuit." He did not add the customary "please."

"Indeed." The plate was passed without apparent notice of Papa's rudeness. "Margaret, dear?"

Now. Say it now.

"No more, thanks." She turned to Mr. Blake. "Sir, I require a moment with you privately."

"At this moment?"

"I believe this is as good a time as any."

"Do you know what she wants?" he asked Robert.

"No, sir. I do not." Robert examined her closely.

"Since this is a family occasion, I see no reason not to speak right here," Mr. Blake stated firmly.

"Very well. I think Papa should work again in our shop, sir."

"What?" Robert yelped.

"I think it would help my father if his time were occupied gainfully. And, of course, I will help him."

"Wait! Wait!" cried Mr. Blake, the veins on his temples swelling. The room quieted. "Mr. Roberge, sir, can you comment on this plan of your daughter's?"

"What plan?" her father asked.

"I thought it would be jolly if you and I worked in the store, like Mama and I used to do," Margaret told him.

His face crumpled. "Your mother is dead."

"Yes, Papa. But I am not."

"That's right!" he exclaimed.

"I could take her place, down at the store. And you could manage it."

"Perhaps I should!" Papa looked around the room, bright as a bird.

"Prepostrous. Our sort do not work in stores, Miss Margaret," Mr. Blake pronounced.

There it was, right out in the open. She must tread carefully.

"My father seems rather taken by the idea, Mr. Blake. Perhaps an exception could be made. For a while, sir."

"I am non-plussed," Blake declared. "Non-plussed."

Mrs. Blake intervened. "This dear child has been through so much! Does she even understand what she's saying? Does it matter? No! What matters are the nuptuals."

"What nuptuals?" Papa asked.

"We have committed ourselves to maintaining Roberge Imports ourselves. Its income guarantees our ability to take care of your father properly," Mr. Blake said, without answering Papa's question. "So that he may continue living in the manner to which we wish he would become accustomed."

"What does that mean?" Papa wondered aloud. "Margaret will see to it that I am comfortable."

A long pause ensued.

"We must think about this carefully. If you wish your father to be a common vender," Mr. Blake began, "then your position in our family . . ."

"I'm getting a headache," Robert complained.

"Darling boy, do take Miss Roberge down to the wharf," Madam Blake begged. "Margaret, my dear, a cargo of silks and satins arrived only yesterday. You might like to take a look and see if there's anything you'd like to have made up for yourself. We can discuss the nuptuals when you get back," she went on. "Assuming we can clear up this nonsense about you running your shop with your father."

"What nuptuals?" Papa asked again.

"Margaret and Robert's."

"You're getting married, Meg?" he asked. "Aren't you a little young?"

"I believe it would help Papa to regain the clarity he has so obviously lost," Margaret persisted, "Once he is immersed in the business he knows so well, his memory may return."

"I think Robert should take Miss Margaret to see the silks. Now." Mrs. Blake was equally persistent. "With less confusion, perhaps our dear Mr. Roberge will be able to tell us if he would enjoy working the shop."

"What shop?" Papa asked.

"My God, my God, why hast thou forsaken me," blasphemed Mr. Blake, his eyes closed, face tilted up to the ceiling.

"Miss Margaret?" Robert asked in a soothing, placating voice, as though he were speaking to someone demented. "Would you do me the honor of walking with me?"

"It would be my pleasure, sir!"

Anything was better than the craziness in this parlor.

"I'll come back for you, darling Papa."

At the front door, Robert said, "You understand, of course, that the shipment is one of tea only."

"Tea only?" She frowned.

"As far as the customs house is concerned."

"Ah, Of course!" The silks and satins would not be included in the ship's manifest, thus entering the colonies duty-free. Already they were hidden in the Blake warehouse.

Offering his arm, he said, "It's such a pleasant day. Let us could stroll up Pemberton Hill first. Observe the waterfront from afar. Put this business nonsense out of our heads."

"That would be pleasant," she agreed, and they walked toward the smaller hill that defined the shape of downtown Boston. A set of stone steps initiated the pathway to the top. A stray whiff of fetid air from the tidal basin nudged their nostrils.

"We'll get used to it in a bit."

"Yes, of course." Everyone always did. There was little choice in the matter. Twice a day low tide prevailed in the Back Bay.

There was a small clearing beside the path that provided for a respite, and they stopped to look out over the water, glittering like strewn shillings in the sun; the gulls squawked in their unending conversations.

No one was near.

"Can you find it in your heart to love me?" he asked. "That's what I really want to know, Miss Margaret."

He had never been so direct before. "Well, well, sir, I'm sure I will when I get to know you better."

"I feel that you are quite distracted," he complained. "As though avoiding me."

"I'm very sorry," she soothed. "I did not realize . . . perhaps it is what might be expected . . ." She gestured toward her somber black dress.

"How thoughtless of me!" he exclaimed. "Let us not dwell on that aspect of our friendship just now. Forgive my being impetuous!"

"Of course," she assured him.

"But perhaps we had better clear up this business situation, Margaret, my dear."

"Of course."

"Do you plan to stand behind the counter at your store and sell things even after we marry?"

"Good grief, Mr. Blake! How could you think such a thing!"

"I hope I haven't offended you, dear Margaret. It is only that I have not known a woman in business. You wouldn't wear breeches, would you?"

"Oh, Robert, how droll!" she laughed, and the two of them giggled for a while, picturing Margaret in clothing meant for a man. Robert, of course, did not know that she had worn leggings or breeches during much of her stay in Acadia.

She smiled obliquely at him, and he took her hand. "Perhaps I could kiss your cheek. By way of getting to know you better."

"Very well," she murmured, and he proceeded to do so. Then his lips traveled down the side of her face, to her neck, throat, and threatened to explore lower.

"My cheek is not down there, sir."

Stepping back, he bowed. "I think apologies are in order. Please accept mine."

"Of course," she nodded graciously. "Perhaps it's time to go to the warehouse. And look! There's the Halifax Packet, coming in." She pointed out over the harbor. "We can find out if it has brought any news."

"Yes, I suppose we can," he agreed without enthusiasm.

Long Wharf was nothing more and nothing less than a long, broad avenue that was a continuation of King Street, with buildings on each side containing offices, counting houses, shops and warehouses. Ships were tied up bow to stern, waiting to have their cargoes taken off and new ones put on. Blake's establishment was in the middle, and the ship that Blake senior had talked of was secured there, its fore and aft gangplanks connecting it to its warehouse.

The packet was tied up at the end of the wharf, rather than anchoring at a mooring and bringing its officers in by dory.

"It must have cargo," Margaret remarked, shading her eyes so to see it more clearly.

"Most likely." Robert squinted at it. He was quite myopic.

"Let's go take a look," she urged, and hurried him down the hill, down King Street, out onto the wharf and Blake's offices. Stopping there to catch their breath, they heard a drum roll, and then the unison step of soldiers who marched past them. In their wake paraded the secretary to the governor, carrying a large ledger, a handful of his clerks bearing pens, ink, and papers, and four burly men carrying a large table and two substantial wooden chairs. Behind them a multitude of Boston tradesmen and dockworkers and loiterers followed curiously.

"Let's see what's happening, Robert!" Taking his hand, Margaret pulled him along with the crowd. At the end of the wharf more soldiers, who had been on board the ship, were already running out the gangplank.

The government's procession was called to a halt. Unintelligible orders were given. Some of the governor's redcoats formed a pathway from the gangplank to the table and chairs now in place, while others fanned out so that no one disembarking could run away. The crowd closed in behind them. A man just in back of Robert said, "Damn Frogs. This'll show 'em."

Robert turned. "McCardy! Tom McCardy!" He thrust out a hand. "Good to see you, sir!"

"Hey! It's Robert Blake! Here, sir, Let me introduce my new business partner."

The men bowed to one another. Margaret, who had turned at these greetings, glanced up at Robert, inviting him to introduce her. More bows, sweepings of tri-cornered hats.

"Do you know of this matter?" she asked them, trying to sound naïve and in need of their help.

"The ship is carrying French people, from Nova Scotia," the man named McCardy told her. "They are enemies of the crown. They have refused to sign the oath of allegiance to His Majesty and some of them have even fought with the French. They're lucky their heads are still attached to their bodies, damn them. Pardon my language, Mistress."

"I must warn you that Miss Margaret is French," Robert grinned at McCardy.

"You called them frogs," reminded the second man to the first.

"Oh, dear," McCardy said, dismayed. "If I have offended you, Miss . . ."

"I am American," she curtseyed. "Call them whatever you like. But why are they here?"

"This is just the first shipment. Governor Shirley plans to deport them all eventually, to one colony or another, all spread out so they can't band together and continue their work against us," Tom McCardy informed them.

Others in the crowd turned to listen while everyone waited for the Acadians to appear. The secretary opened his large ledger

CHAPTER TEN

and placed it on the table. The quills, ink, and extra paper were arranged close at hand. The clerks hovered.

"Easier to just throw 'em overboard," Robert said to his friends. "And cheaper. Now the crown will have to feed them."

Thomas McCardy laughed sardonically. "I'm afraid someone will have to, but it won't be His Majesty. It'll be us. Governor Shirley has decreed that the towns will have to support them."

"Ah, so it's all Governor Shirley's idea!" The new business partner seemed impressed. "A decisive fellow, I would guess."

"He's going to deport them?" Margaret asked. "All of them?" A heaviness gathered deep within.

"I believe so."

The drummer stopped. The captain of the vessel appeared on the quarterdeck with papers in his hand. He crossed the gangplank without even looking down to make sure he wouldn't fall in, and approached the governor's secretary. The two men bowed, shook hands, and the captain rounded the table, took the second chair and spread out his notes.

On board the ship, undistinguishable orders were called out. At the top of the gangplank a soldier shouted, and from the hatchway ladder a man appeared, shielding his eyes from the sun. Slowly, very slowly, women with babies in arms and older children were hoisted out and onto the deck, and then more men, some helping elderly people, climbed out of the hold. Their faces were frozen in fear.

On her far side, Tyler Moore murmured, "Good day, Mistress."

Tyler!

He looked wonderful despite ink smudges on his face. "Good day, sir!" she gasped. Thank goodness for her bonnet, the rim of which hid her lips. Robert would never know she was even speaking. "I'm so glad to see you!" She had not laid eyes on him since their meeting in the shed.

Moore's mouth curled up in one corner. "You're here with your beloved, I see. Or, at least, one of them. Mayhap the other is on yonder boat." He nodded toward the schooner.

It was a cruel remark, and they both knew it. "Why are you here, Tyler?"

"I'm presently in the capacity of a journalist. Gathering information about the Acadians. Mr. Adams wants articles written about their plight. And about the mercilessness of our governor. Another example of what happens when officialdom makes decisions about His Majesty's subjects."

Margaret quickly glanced around to see if anyone had heard. But the Acadians were preparing to come ashore now, moving toward the gangplank, and the attention of the crowd was on them.

"Since you've met some of them first hand, Mistress, perhaps you'd describe your impression of them. How much of a threat do they pose, in your opinion?"

"Please, Tyler . . ."

"I won't identify you, if that's got you worried. What Mr. Adams wants to do is point out how heartless our government can be. He thinks it's a lesson we can all benefit from learning." He avoided looking at her, instead was watching the refugees. "The crown will be just as ruthless with us, one day, if we try to oppose its dictates."

Samuel Adams again, though unnamed.

"The Acadians are farmers," she insisted, "just as many of us are." The first of them had reached the secretary's table. The ship's captain looked through his papers, found the correct name. The secretary inscribed it in the ledger, being careful to spell it correctly.

"La Porte?" she heard him ask. "With or without an 'e' on the end."

The captain put him on the right path. All of the names would be written in the ledger so there would be an official record of the deported prisoners. In other the other colonies, identical cargoes would be similarly identified.

"I am glad to see you, Tyler," she murmured shyly.

"And I'm glad to see you," he said, meeting her eyes at last. "Are you well? I see you are wearing mourning."

"For my mother. It puts off the necessity of having to make any decisions for a while, aside from being the correct thing to do."

"So you are not yet engaged?"

"Not yet."

The drummers started up again, and onlookers were silenced. Official pronouncements were made which they could not hear, and the soldiers formed a guard around the prisoners, wedging them into a line. The women started to wail and the children cried. A translator told them what the pronouncements had been about and what the soldiers were doing. They quieted and the redcoats cleared the way. They began to move past the officials and through the crowd that lined the route, its murmurs growing and swelling into jeers.

Tyler was gone in an instant. Robert reached for Margaret's hand. "It might get ugly," he cautioned.

As the Acadians passed, Margaret's heart went out to them, so lost, so worried, so downtrodden, and wondered if any were from the Fort Lawrence encampment. But none of the faces were familiar—except—except that one! That one approaching now—that one at the end of the line, coming closer . . .

"Armand!" she shrieked. "Armand St. Martin!"

The crowd quieted. She pushed forward. "Armand!"

St. Martin, dirty and downcast, looked around when he heard his name, found her.

But he did not call back. Instead, looked at her with pleading, anguished eyes and then passed by. Around her, strangers gawked.

Robert was astonished. "You know that fellow?"

"Indeed I do!" Her heart was hammering loudly. "He was one of the men who helped me get to the English fort. He saved my life," she explained to anyone who would listen.

"Then we owe him a debt of gratitude," Robert said graciously.

"Indeed we do!" The plan bloomed before her eyes, like a rose in June. "Robert, might your parents provide shelter for some of the Acadians at your country estate?"

"At Mystic Meadow?" he frowned. "Keep Acadians at Medfield?"

"Yes, yes! It could support any number of them, and they could help clear it and chop down trees and, and . . . They could start the formal gardens that you and your parents have planned. The ones we were going to lay out this Sunday. That your father was going to hire slave labor for next spring."

"These Acadians—are they willing workers?"

"They are farmers, Robert. They can do whatever is needed, and grow their own food besides. They could even plant late vegetables now, and if your father wanted to breed livestock, they could attend to the animals and help birth new ones."

"Would they be willing?" he asked, an acquisitive look in his eyes. The Blakes were ever ready to take advantage of a situation.

"Of course they would. It would mean they could stay together, instead of being scattered here and there, too far apart to comfort each other. They would be grateful to you, Robert! They'd do anything you asked. Quickly, let's go back to your house and see if your father agrees, and if he will petition the governor for a number of them."

"Where will they sleep?"

"They can build themselves shelters. Believe me, they know how! When they're done with that, they can clear the fields and open up riding paths in the woods for your family's guests."

Her color was high, her shoulders straight, her expression animated in a manner Robert had not seen since her return six weeks ago. If this is what it took to make her happy, he was not averse to it; her proposal would benefit the Blakes, after all, and the Acadians would not be there, at Mystic Meadow, forever. They could be shipped elsewhere any time they became burdensome.

"Very well," he smiled, and was rewarded by the expression of gratitude on her face, which he took to be admiration. This was more like it! "You'd have to be the go-between with the Acadians and us. We'll have to see what my father thinks about it. But the idea has possibilities, Margaret, it truly does."

And if they—and Armand St. Martin—could lead her to Marc Duval, and if indeed he loved her as he had said he did, perhaps there was a chance—for what, she did not know. But she would fain find out. He had taught her to love, to live the present, to be open to whatever came her way. And just now? It was these Acadians....

She would talk to Armand. She would find out if he knew where Marc was, and if there might be a chance to see him again. Would Armand even know?

Armand always knew.

Always.

CHAPTER
11

Mystic Meadow

The Medfield village bell rang insistently, on and on, notifying the faithful that it was time for Meeting. The Blakes' carriage was brought around, and everyone climbed in—Robert, his parents, and herself. The Blakes, after all, were Medford's gentry, and must appear at Meeting whenever they were at Mystic Meadow. They were not Congregationalists; they attended the Anglican Church in Boston, along with the Upper Orders. But there was protocol to follow.

Behind, in back of the mansion, the Acadians prayed the rosary.

It had been a busy and productive week. Within a day of having seen Armand, she had secured the support of the Blakes and they, in turn, of the Lt. Governor, who had no idea what to do with the prisoners. Gladly did he give permission for their removal from the Common, where they were camped. They could wait in Medfield until Governor Shirley decided what to do with them when he returned.

Margaret assembled her best friends and persuaded them to mount the "Acadian Endeavour". It would give the wealthy an opportunity to Do Good to those who hated them, as advised by the Good Book. And it gave the girls the chance to enter the homes of Boston's well-to-do, begging for cast-off clothing for the refugees. No one wanted to miss out on that! Nor, of course, the chance to Do Good, as was expected of unmarried girls. They canvassed the upper class in pairs, and then those of a lesser caste, and then the more moderately comfortable families, like their own.

Later in the week, the donations were packed up, stowed aboard *HMSSudley*, borrowed from His Majesty whose ships were always to be found loitering about the harbor. The refugees were onloaded, followed by six red coated guards.

The women and children went below. The guards clustered at the bow, the Acadian men at the stern while Margaret and Armand talked loudly enough in French for them to hear and be reassured that there were no nefarious plans afoot.

"How can we thank you, *Mademoiselle*," Armand said, bowing.

The listening men bowed, too.

"Your benefactors, the Blakes, need a great deal of work done on their land. I have told them that these men can cut down trees and make firewood for export."

"Surely," he nodded. "Unfortunately there are only ten, as you see." He gestured at them. "Many are hiding and have escaped capture. They are working with the Acadian underground. But the men here, family men, did not flee. And they are good workers." The men bowed again. "They will cut trees down—the ones that Lord Blake wishes cut, and once the tree is down, they will use the branches to make wetu's, if that meets with the approval of the lord."

"We do not have lords, Armand. Mr. Blake is simply rich enough to buy land and put a house on it for his pleasure, and that of his guests. What is a wetu?"

"The kind of shelter made by natives here in Massachusetts and elsewhere in New England. Unlike the Mi'kmaqs, they do not use tipis. I know not why."

She burned to ask him about Marc, and he knew it, yet there was no opportunity here and now. She must, somehow, make one.

Obediently the Acadians had disembarked at Mystic Meadow, all hands helping to unload the provisions and take them into the house or stack them in the barn. With her help, Mr. Blake showed Armand where trees might be cut for export. The rest of the men disappeared to find enough fallen branches to build temporary shelters. The women unpacked flour and bread starter and cornmeal and haunches of ham; a butter churn and cheese press were among the items brought over from Boston, and the women were introduced to the three cows that lived in the barn, along with the horses that pulled the coach.

His Majesty's ship left with the tide, gruel was cooked and served and the Acadians prepared themselves to sleep on the ground as they had on the Common. Exhausted, the Blake entourage retired upstairs to the chambers of the house, the servants to the attic.

The Acadians were up at dawn this morning, Sunday, their subdued chatter humming like bees at a hive. The Blakes' staff served breakfast as best they could, working around the piles of supplies now cluttering the kitchen, and then the family, along with Margaret, rode away in style. Armand was nowhere to be seen; Margaret was frantic with the need to speak with him before the afternoon tide, when the family would depart on their little schooner *Robin*, brought in on the night tide for that purpose.

The church bell was still ringing when the coach pulled up and the driver opened the door, lowered the little steps that would allow the passengers to dismount. Entering the simple and unadorned Meeting House, the Blakes nodded a greeting at the selectmen and the fence viewer and the pound keeper and the hog reeve as they filed into their pew and settled themselves for the boring morning.

"Are you familiar with the order of worship here?" Margaret whispered to Robert.

"We just do what everyone else does."

She nodded.

The bell stopped ringing and the minister entered. Everyone rose. The Reverend Marshall Dimock marched to the front and up the three stair steps to the pulpit, turned, arms outstretched. He was a large bull of a man, with huge hands, broad shoulders, and a short torso, making him resemble a black robed barrel. His waving mane of hair, white as snow, was tied behind by a black grosgrain ribbon. Clean shaven, stock immaculate, fingers ink-stained, he was exactly the image of the village minister and guardian of the church.

"This is the day the Lord hath made," he announced.

"Let us rejoice and be glad in it," the congregation responded, and Dimock lowered his arms. The gathering reseated itself with a great bustling.

"Welcome, one and all—brothers and sisters in the Lord!"

The service had begun.

"We are happy to see Squire and Madam Blake with us this morning." He bowed in their direction, and the Blakes nodded their response. "And their son. And their guest."

Margaret nodded also, feeling conspicuous. Robert seemed quite at ease with being singled out, as though it were his due.

"I am informed that Squire Blake is providing shelter for a group of French refugees." He glanced at Robert's father, who stood up, bowed to the Congregation, sat again. "The refugees will stay on the Blake's estate, They are guarded by His Majesty's troops, and you have nothing to fear from them. Let us pray."

CHAPTER ELEVEN

As one, the congregation popped up again, their hinged seats clattering against the backs of their pews as they did so. They closed their eyes, held their chins up high. Bowing the head during prayer was redolent of Popery, but the Blakes, being Anglican, did it anyway. Caught in the middle, Margaret simply stared at the pew ahead and hoped for the best.

"Lord, we thank thee that our honorable governor has acted vigorously to save us from the depredations of the Acadians in Nova Scotia."

Good grief! Depredations? Margaret glared up at the minister, who did not notice, his eyes being closed.

"We thank you, Lord, that you have shown us, through this action of the governor, that indeed we are your chosen people despite our losses to the French further south. We pray that you will continue to bless us despite our errors."

What losses further south? Margaret wondered.

Dimock proceeded to enumerate the errors committed, in case the congregation had forgotten what they were. When they had been thoroughly chastened in the form of prayer, he paused, and paused longer, and longer still. The sick and elderly, knowing their release had come, fell into their hinged seats gratefully.

Dimock continued.

"Lord, it is nearly certain that we are going to have yet another war with the French. His Majesty sent one of his greatest officers, His Excellency General Edward Braddock, along with troops, to join and lead the Virginia militia and make it clear that the French must abandon the forts they have built on the Western Frontier. This officer has died in battle. Thus, war is inevitable.

"The Indians will be in the middle of this white man's conflict. We ask, O Lord, if it is Thy desire, that we show them the way, the truth, and the light as did our beloved John Eliot, so they will refrain from lifting their hands against us and also, so that they will enter the gates of heaven."

John Eliot.

His Praying Indians had been decimated more than 75 years ago, victims of an Indian uprising against the white man. Little, if any, missionary work had been done since that time.

"If it is God's will, we shall go into the wilderness as did John the Baptist!" Dimock's voice rose to clarion pitch. "We shall make straight the way of the Lord and continue the work of John Eliot. Speak to us, Heavenly Father! Show us what we must do. Amen. The congregation will be seated."

So stunned, both by Dimock's fervor and by the threat of seeking out the dreaded Indian, that there was a long moment before all the hinged seats dropped as one, resounding like thunder in the stillness of the morning.

The tithingman turned the hourglass.

A deacon in the front row rose to face the congregation. "We shall praise the Lord in song."

Again they stood. The deacon intoned the first line of the psalm: *My voice you shall hear in the morning, O Lord.*

In unison, they all repeated his drone in varying pitches.

In the morning I will look up and know,

. . . and know, they droned loudly.

that the Lord has set apart for himself

. . . for himself

he who is godly.

The volume was building.

Make a joyful noise unto the Lord.

MAKE A JOYFUL NOISE UNTO THE LORD.

The cacophony rose to the rafters. The Congregation seated itself without being told to do so. Another Deacon mounted the pulpit to read Scripture.

Then it was time for the sermon. Dimock preached for the next two hours about John Eliot and his Praying Indians, all of whom had rudely been exiled to George's Island when King Philip led his warriors against the whites, both to protect them from their own kind, who considered them traitors, and to make sure they didn't change their minds and join the uprising. Many of them died there of exposure and disease.

Allowing her mind to wander, Margaret thought about her Acadians. They had been taken near Grand Pré, she had learned, even though they were willing to swear the oath of allegiance. Too late. Many more would follow, caught and crowded onto ships and peddled up and down the coast, perhaps even taken to England. It was a disaster of the greatest proportion.

"Please rise for the benediction," Dimock announced. Everyone stood up, covertly glancing at one another as their pastor, with upraised hand and outstretched arm, blessed them and sent them on their way to the tavern to eat a noon meal, or to the homes of friends who lived nearby, returning to church when summoned by the bell for the afternoon service.

Which the Blakes, being Anglican, would not attend.

"Incredible," Robert declared on the ride back home. "This business of converting the Indians."

"I am surprised that the minister would take it upon himself to launch such an initiative," observed his father.

"Doesn't a synod or church council have to approve?" asked Mrs. Blake.

"Each congregation decides its own path", Margaret told them. "If Mr. Dimock's parish doesn't support his call to action, he can either resign and take on the mission he proposes by himself, or simply be given a leave of absence while he explores the possibilities."

The cook and her staff had prepared a simple dinner, and the dining room had been readied in the absence of the family.

After changing into more suitable garments, they filed in and seated themselves. The maid, Sofie, brought in the soup tureen. "We've prepared small, stuffed game hens for the main course, Madam, with glazed carrots. Shall I bring them in after the soup, or now?"

"Perhaps now," Mrs. Blake directed. "We must be ready to return at about—3:00, dear?"

Mr. Blake, dishing out the soup, nodded. "So I was told by the men who brought *Robin* up last night."

The front door knocker rattled.

They all looked at one another in surprise. The Blakes had no friends in Medfield.

"Take care of it, Sofie, and then bring the hens."

"Yes, ma'am." The girl disappeared.

"Good day to you," trumpeted the baritone of Reverend Dimock. "I should like to speak to Mr. Blake."

"He is at dinner, sir."

"Oh, gracious!" Quickly Mrs. Blake pushed back her chair and hurried into the foyer.

"Welcome, sir!"

"Madam." The minister bowed.

"As the girl said, we were just gathering for dinner. Will you join us?"

"Madam, there are only four hens," protested the girl.

"No matter. Miss Margaret and I will share one."

"Very kind of you, Madam. I know it is an imposition, but there is no other time . . ." He followed her.

The men rose, bowed, fetched an extra chair. Another bowl of soup was produced.

"Please forgive my intrusion," Dimock said as he spooned in his dinner. "I get hungry when I preach," he explained, accepting another bowl which effectively used up what was left. "I do want to tell you how commendable I think it is, that you are sheltering these Papist foreigners," he said between mouthfuls. "The villagers believe it's tantamount to aiding and abetting the enemy, but since I do not, there have been no objections."

"How nice." Mrs. Blake smiled sweetly.

"Especially since we'd have done so, regardless," added Mr. Blake. He, too, smiled—not so sweetly. The opinion of the masses was of no significance to him. "After all, if it weren't for the Acadians, our dear friend here might never have made it home," he amended, so that he sounded less churlish.

"Well, sir, now that you bring it up, it is the young lady I wish to speak with. I understand she knows French."

"As do I," Robert intervened. "Mother and Father are conversant, too, if not fluent."

"You never know when we might go back home to England, and be presented at court," Mrs. Blake spoke firmly about this possibility. "They speak French there."

The habits of royalty were unknown to Dimock, nor did they hold interest for him. "Mistress Roberge's rescue surely is evidence of the grace of God," he said. "I am hopeful that, with the help of that grace, she and her Acadian friends can help facilitate my plan."

"Plan?"

"To preach to the Indians, sir. As I talked about all morning. I need the young lady's assistance."

"Surely you are jesting. Why would a lovely young woman want to trek through the Massachusetts wilderness, having just been returned from Nova Scotia?"

"I do not wish her to accompany me," Dimock protested. "Only to help me find someone who can."

Apparently it was now her turn to speak; everyone was looking at her.

To Robert's mother, she said, "Perhaps you'd rather we excused ourselves, the Reverend and I. So that your repast is uninterrupted."

"No, no," Mr. Blake waved a hand. "We are somewhat in the position of being your guardian while you are here, Miss Roberge. Any plan Rev. Dimock has in mind needs our approval. Do you agree, Mrs. Blake?"

"Yes, yes, I suppose." The issue had never come up before.

"Well, then, sir, we await your words!" Mr. Blake waved a hand.

"Miss, your Acadians have lived among the natives for many years, and I understand Indians get along better with the French than they do with the English. And the Acadians are French."

"That is true, they are." She smiled at the obtuseness of this country minister.

"I have a copy of Reverend Eliot's Bible," Dimock announced. "As you probably know, Reverend Eliot had to invent a written language that sounds like Indian speech. I have learned how to read it, but I do not know how to pronounce it, thus I cannot preach to the Indians. Miss Roberge, do you think there might be an Acadian who could tutor me?"

Clearly he meant to go into the wilderness by himself.

"Any language they might know would be the one spoken by the Mi'kmaqs, sir," she managed to say around her astonishment at his ignorance. "Their language is a different dialect, I am sure, than the one spoken here."

"That's exactly right. Eliot's Bible is a written version of the Abanaki language. But both the Abanaki and the Mi'kmaq are dialects of the Algonquian language. I thought—I hoped—there might be enough similarity . . ."

The tureen and soup bowls were taken away by the maid. The hens arrived, and a gravy boat, and the glazed carrots. Furor arose while one of the hens was divided, stuffing doled out, gravy flooding all, and more biscuits, and while it was going on, Margaret had a chance to think.

The *coureurs du bois* and the *voyageurs* necessarily picked up the languages of the tribes with whom they traded, at least in a rudimentary sense, sometimes fluently.

A tiny spark fell on a small piece of tinder in the back of her brain.

"So your, er, Acadian guests will not know the language of the Indians here, in Massachusetts Bay Colony?" Dimock asked.

"They do not. But a *coureur du bois* might. Or a *voyageur*."

"Coureur du bois? Voyageur?"

"A fur traders . . . They are Frenchmen who collect pelts from the natives for use in France. It's a very lucrative trade, and they travel widely, trade with all Indian nations, and get along well with all kinds of natives."

The tinder flared up, then subsided in a curl of smoke.

"Do you know of such a man?"

"I do not. But there is someone here who might."

"Here?" exclaimed Mrs. Blake.

"Who?" asked Mr. Blake.

"Armand St. Martin. We plan to use him here as a supervisor," Margaret explained to Dimock, "to translate the requirements of the estate to the refugees. He cannot travel with you, because he is a prisoner of war, but perhaps he can locate a person who knows the language of Massachusetts, since he knows all the *coureurs du bois* and *voyageurs*."

The tiny heap was carefully fanned; more tinder was added.

"Can you ask this St. Martin fellow now?" Dimock inquired.

"I'd be glad to."

The tinder burst into flame.

Mrs. Blake intervened. "We'll be leaving within the hour."

"Let me at least try," she said, pushing her chair back. "If Armand can find a trader, then he could arrange for me to meet him, and if he seems adequate, I can introduce him to you, Reverend."

Dimock dissolved into tears of gratitude. "God bless you," he sobbed, also pushing back his chair. "I must go back for afternoon Meeting now. I will tell the congregation that I may, myself, be able to answer the call."

"You wish to create praying towns, as Eliot did?" Robert asked as the minister edged his way around the table, heading for the door.

"That would be my goal. As I announced this morning, I have been called," Dimock said through his beatific tears. "I shall start with simply bringing the Indians to Christ. The rest will take care of itself, if that is the will of God," he called over his shoulder. The door slammed shut behind him.

As one, the Blakes turned to her, curious about what she might do next, and Margaret, excusing herself, hurried into the kitchen and out the back door, toward a triad of men who were finishing up a wetu.

"*Ou est Armand St. Martin?*" she asked the men. Where is Armand St. Martin?

They looked at one another, then at her, and said nothing.

"*Je connais sais qu'il est ici.*" I know he is here.

Still they only stared.

"May I remind you that it is by my intercession you are not in a prison on Castle Island?" she snapped.

Quickly they conferred and one detached himself, disappearing into the woods where sounds of chopping and sawing could be heard.

"There's not much time," she called after him, and turned toward the river and the dock where *Robin* bobbed with the current. The meadow was full of wild flowers, lovely and lively in their own unadorned way.

"*Mademoiselle Marguerite?*"

She looked around and there he was. He bowed and she dipped him a small curtsey of greeting. "Oh, Armand!"

"Are you well, *Mademoiselle?*"

"I am. And you?"

"*Moi aussi.*" He nodded.

"You and I have not had a chance to speak privately yet, and I hope that soon we will. If you can help me, I'll be able to stay here for a bit, and we can talk as much as we want."

"That would be quite wonderful," he smiled. "These English people would leave you behind?"

"If I can persuade them. After all, there are six soldiers here. What harm could possibly come to me?"

"What is the help you need?"

"The minister of the Medfield church—here in town— wishes to convert the natives to Christianity."

He shrugged. "It is always thus with men of the cloth. Priests are no different."

"In order to convert them, he needs to speak their language."

"*Bien sur.*" Certainly.

"And maybe you know someone who has traded in this area, and who knows the tongue. Perhaps knows it very well, having been raised among the Maleseet in Maine."

Armand began to smile. "All tribes of the Algonquian nation are able to understand one another, if they try hard enough. But Malacite is particularly compatible with the language spoken here."

She waited.

His expression was bland. "How long will you linger?"

"I have not arranged that detail. I needed to see you first. The Blakes are returning to Boston today with the ebb-tide. I hope to remain behind for a day or so."

"Tell me what is your position with these people, the Blakes."

"They think I'm going to marry their son, Robert."
"And does their son believe this also?"
"I think he does."
"And are you? Going to marry him?"
"Not if I can help it," she smiled.

Armand looked at her long and steadily. "Very well," he said. "I will bring the person you need here, tomorrow morning."

"*Bien.* I'm sure I can convince the Blakes to leave me here for one single day."

He nearly laughed. "Perhaps you will need more, *Mademoiselle*. Perhaps you will wish more. Why be so definite?"

"Armand!" she giggled, poking him. "You are bad. Very, very bad."

"It is in the eye of the beholder, is it not?" he retorted, and left to resume the trimming of trees.

The sun embraced the back garden as the Acadian women, sitting on horse blankets, altered the clothing donations to meet the needs of the refugees. Margaret sewed among them. On one side of her a woman took in the seams of a pair of satin breeches with gold buttons on them. They would be made over for an Acadian boy who had never in his life seen such splendor.

On the other side a matron enlarged a pair of woolen breeches, inserting embroidered bell pulls along the edges of each leg to increase their girth. One of the men would have very beautiful breeches, and probably his friends would tease him unmercifully until they, too, were outfitted with new clothes of surprising design.

They all heard the voices—and of course they all understood, because Armand was speaking French.

CHAPTER ELEVEN

"*Cette maison*—this house—belongs to the family that thinks she is going to marry their son."

There came silence. A protracted silence. An expectant silence, into which a voice she believed she would never hear again asked, also in French, "This house will be Marguerite's, if she marries his man?"

"*Non*. It is the property of the father."

They came around the corner of the house, into the sunshine, and finally she was able to see him, his wonderful face, his broad shoulders, his lean hips and long boot-covered legs. Bronzed from the summer's sun, wearing a baggy shirt like Acadian farmers wore, his gaze burned bright.

Her work—a shift edged with lace made out of a former table cloth—slid to the ground as she jumped up and out of the circle.

His deep and infinitely tender eyes told her of his love as he took her hand, brought it to his lips. "Marguerite," he murmured, and she fell back into the special place where nothing existed but the two of them. Oh, yes, she was glad she had prepared for this meeting in the special way of women.

How she had survived their parting at all?

"Where shall we discuss the proposal the Domanie wishes to make?" Marc asked.

"There is a stable yonder," Armand said, pointing. "Perhaps you would wish to speak inside? All the animals are out to pasture."

"Let us be quick about it," Marc grinned, and they walked there with him. Behind her, she heard one of the women say: *J'ai entendu dire qu'elle est la putain of de Marc Duval*. I've heard she is Marc Duvan's whore. Another bid the speaker to shut her mouth.

Armand tactfully disappeared as soon as they entered the barn's dimness, dust modes drifting about in shafts of sunlight and the sweet scent of hay everywhere. Instantly they were in each other's arms, kissing, kissing, devouring: face, throat, mouth. O, Marc Duval! She could not get enough of him, could not embrace him as fully as she must. Having him back, even for a flash, was to know how truly empty was her life without him.

They parted at arms length, catching their breath.

His eyes consumed her. "I have never seen you dressed like a lady," he breathed. "We should have carried you in a sedan chair, instead of making you haul packs. You were too good for us."

She laughed, joyous for the first time since he'd left her. "And believe me, I had imagined myself being carried in a chair! With curtains, if you please!" She held her skirt out and brushed its hem forward and back.

"Will you forgive us? Forgive me?" His eyes were so deep she was endlessly lost in his gaze.

"Your men would have mutinied if they'd had to tote me in a chair." She reached around his lean waist and clasped her hands behind him, leaned her head against his chest. His heart was beating as fast as her own.

"Tote?"

"Another word for carry."

"Ah, to tote. To carry." He lifted her up. "Like this? I tote you—to—that pile of hay."

He carried her there. "Marguerite, Marguerite, Marguerite, my Singing Bird." His hand sought her breast urgently, and discovered she was wearing nothing beneath her kerchief and short gown. Clearly there would be nothing besides the single petticoat tied around her waist, either. "You are waiting for me."

"I am."

He looked around the place, saw the ladder leaning against the loft.

"Yes?" he asked, nodding his head in that direction.

"Yes," she whispered. "Let us be quick about it."

Recognizing his own words, he laughed and held out his hand for hers, followed her closely up the ladder and when they were safely ensconsed in the hay, tore his clothing off as she did her own. They came together without even a moments pause. Into her woman-place he plunged and both of them shuddered as she met him and as he drew back and then, oh yes, thrust forward and back—

There was no time—or need—for play. Muffling their cries as best they could, they surged over the edge of reality and grasped the stars of climax, clinging to one another until slowly reality returned and they were alone in their own world, and the loft, and their love.

"As you see, my darling, I have not forgotten how to savor the moment."

"I thought we would not ever be together again," he told her. "Do not the English have a fable in which a prince is restored with a kiss?"

"Yes," she giggled. "But he was disguised as a frog. You definitely do not qualify. You are not green. Oh, Marc, Marc . . ."

He rolled over to face her, his voice unsteady. "Will you forgive my stupidity? I have never loved anyone before, so I understood not what it would be like to part. I should have made a plan to see you again, somewhere, somehow, so that some of the pain could have been contained."

"We'll make a plan now," she soothed reaching out so that she could hold him closer. "I love you. And we are together. Come, lie here quietly while you can."

"Would you have come to me? If I had been wise enough to make a plan?" he asked, his voice nearly plaintive.

"I would go to the ends of the earth if I knew I could be with you, hold you, love you . . ."

"There is a chance now for us, Marguerite." He brought her lips to his, and when the kiss was done, said, "I must explore the path that the Domanie needs to go. There was once a praying village northwest of here, at the Falls of the Merrimack. The white minister, John Eliot, lived there for a long time, trying to convert the great Passaconaway."

"I have never heard of Passaconaway."

"He was chief sachem—called Sagamore—of all the tribes. A giant of a man. He spoke with the gods and received visions from them. Thus he knew that the white man would prevail in the end. The only hope was to try to get along. And of course, Eliot thought so, too. Your minister might do well at the Falls if he invokes the memory of the great sagamore and his vision of peace, and reminds the natives there that Eliot was Passaconaway's friend."

"Reverend Dimock will be very happy," she sighed, relieved to have conquered that challenge.

"The Pennicook live there now. I must first find out if they will welcome or at least tolerate the Domanie. Once he is settled, and after I have attended to my work at the western forts, you will come away with me."

"I will!" she cried. "But how? Oh, Marc, how?"

"Hear me out, my own Bird. Already I have a plan." He looked away, then back again with an expression of sheepishness that she would never have imagined of him. "When I understood what a lamentable mistake I had made, letting you go, I was determined to change it. My task, for the Commandant at Louisbourg, was to find out about the governor Shirley's plan for the Oswego campaign. I travelled to New York colony and then to Boston to learn the details, and while I was there, I learned about you."

"Me! How?"

"I remembered your telling me about Tyler Moore."

Tyler?

"I needed to know if you had married that man you thought you were going to wed. If you had, after all, there was nothing I could do. But if you had not . . . I pretended interest in Moore's activity."

"In printing?"

"No. In his friends, who follow Samuel Adams. Tyler Moore lives above the printery, in a loft. Did you know this?"

"Yes."

"There is a back door to the shop, with stairs just as the door opens, and his friends go up to the loft."

"I didn't know that," she said. "Does Mr. Adams meet with them there?"

"*Monsieur* Adams? No. He does not. I believe they somewhat fashion their own path. But this path leads to a determination to end British rule of the American colonies. A cause that Mr. Adams also cherishes."

"That is treason," she exclaimed. "Tyler is not a traitor!"

He grinned, "History is written by the winner. Whoever wins is a patriot. Whoever loses is a traitor."

"This is very serious, Marc." She shook her head.

"It is also some distance in the future. Right now, the group simply wishes to keep alive the understanding that rule by Britain will become a sort of slavery. Though taxation. But enough! You must hold off your suitor until winter, and you must make it possible for the Acadians to stay here until then. The Blakes—that is their name, is it not? The Blakes must continue to feel kindly toward them."

"As long as they chop down trees and make bridle paths and timber for export, there is no reason for Mr. Blake to change his mind about them."

"Good. Now. You, Marguerete, must be prepared to come to me at a moments notice. When the time is right, whenever it is, or however inconvenient, you must come."

"Perhaps you learned that I am caring for my father."

"Yes. I understand." He drew a long, sad breath. "He is unwell, your father."

"He seems to have become deranged."

"If you ask, I will plan to bring him with us, but I do not recommend it."

She shook her head. "Thanks. But you're right. He is better now than he has been, but I doubt he'd really understand what we'd be doing, and I expect he wouldn't agree to it even if he did."

"Then you must leave him behind."

"Yes," she said softly. "Yes. But I will prepare for it."

"No one must know why."

"No one will."

How could she just turn her back on Papa and leave him, so helpless . . . unless between now and then she could prepare Lucy to take over the business and Papa's care. Perhaps that would pacify her conscience and she could leave in good faith.

"I will meet your minister tomorrow morning," Marc said. "Tell him that Armand has found me, and he can decide then if I am suitable."

"Very well."

"I will have to pretend I don't know you."

"Yes."

"And you will have to pretend you do not know me."

"I understand," she murmured, feasting her eyes on his face, drawing him close, brushing his chest with her lips, and his throat and then reaching for a farewell kiss . . . Yes, it would work somehow.

Sometimes it didn't pay to think too carefully, too far ahead, until the time came when it was right to do so . . . .

CHAPTER ELEVEN

Dimock was ecstatic. "It's going to work out very well." His eyes twinkled beneath the furry white eyebrows. "When the weather gets cooler, everyone will bring two logs each Sunday, one for morning and one for afternoon service. The deacons will keep everything in order in my absence, and ministers from the nearby towns will take turns supplying the pulpit. They admire me!"

They are glad you are going, Margaret did not say aloud. Then they don't have to ask themselves if they ought to do the same thing. They can say they're already helping, after all, by supplying your pulpit.

At his feet lay his supplies, already packed. Six boxes filled with slates and chalk for the pupils he would teach; writing paper and ink for his memoir and baubles to attract the native women, whom he hoped would coax the men to listen.

"My dear wife will go to live with my eldest son's family in Beverly. They are expecting a baby, and she can help." Impatiently, he looked around as though his guide were hidden behind a nearby tree. "Where is he? What is his name?"

"Etienne del Mar," she told him, the pseudonym that Marc had agreed to use. "He will be here soon."

"The Lord be praised," Dimock intoned. "I can save the noble savage from the errors of the Papist after all."

She nodded piously.

Across the road, the bushes parted: Armand and Marc emerged, both with packs, their leggings and moccasins muddy, as if they had been traveling for several days.

They had not.

"Is that him?" Dimock asked eagerly.

"It is."

Oh, yes, that was him, dressed in Algonquin regalia, complete with green stripes on his cheeks so that Dimock would have trouble recognizing him later on, should their paths cross.

Or was he reminding her of the frog prince? She suppressed a smile.

"*Bonjour*, Mistress Roberge," Armand called.

"*Bonjour*," she returned, with eyes only for Marc, whom she would not see again for an indefinite period of time.

Armand bowed to the Reverend and waved toward his green-painted companion with a sweeping gesture. "*Alors*, Domanie. Here your guide stands. He is Etienne."

Marc and the Reverend eyed one another cautiously.

"I am told you speak English."

"*Oui*," answered Etienne del Mar. Deliberately using broken idiom, he elaborated. "I speak much English." He did not so much as glance Margaret's way. An Indian male, after all, would not lower himself to acknowledge the presence of a white woman.

"And Algonquin?"

"And Algonquin yes, and Micmac and Abnaki. Also Pemiquid and Pawtucket," he added. These were not dialects, but place names. Dimock did not to notice.

"Ideal!" he declared. "And can you find bearers to carry my supplies? I do not think you can manage all the boxes by yourself, boy."

Neither Marc nor Armand so much as flicked an eyelid. "I take you to camp of Sly Fox," Etienne del Mar said. "You speak. I tell him what you say. He speaks. I tell you what he say. If he feel good, he send his women for boxes."

Dimock glanced questioningly at Armand. "I thought we were going to the falls of the Merrimack."

"You must pass through the territory of Sly Fox to get there. And you must have his approval before going on," Armand explained.

"Very well. And if he approves, he will send the ladies back? Why is that? The boxes are very heavy."

"The women do all the lugging. Never the men," Margaret explained. "Some of the chief's braves will accompany the women, but they serve as guards and keep watch for anything that might harm them."

"How far is this village?" Dimock asked.

"Three campfires from here," Marc/Etienne told him, his fluent English now well-transmogrified. "Much to walk."

"I believe His Majesty plans to take the French Fort Niagara. Soon, I think." Dimock asked, "Will combat there interfere with my work?"

"I understand not," Armand said, playing dumb. "What means combat?"

"Fighting, my boy. You know—what they do in a war."

"Fort far away."

"Far enough?" Dimock asked.

Armand and the green painted Indian stared, expressionless.

"He wants to know if there will be fighting anywhere near Sly Fox's village," Margaret intervened. "Whether or not it is safe to be there."

"Already he has been told the answer. Fort is on great lake to the west. Many miles from here, so also many miles from Sly Fox."

"Good!" Dimock's face shone with his smile. He nodded jovially toward Etienne del Mar.

"Haargh!" The Green Man spat into the dust uncomfortabley close to where Dimock stood. "How many packs?"

Dimock looked to Armand.

"Natives, they carry things in packs."

"I do not. I carry mine in boxes."

"Harder."

"Boxes," Dimock repeated. "They can be used to write upon, like a desk. I myself am prepared to make a farewell sermon Sunday and can leave the following Monday, at dawn."

"This is good," Etienne del Mar said to the minister. "I go to Sly Fox, to the Falls, find out if agreeable. Return in five suns." He turned to Armand. "He does not understand French, this Domanie?"

"*Non.*"

"Singing Bird," Duval said, without looking at her. "I have many tasks ahead. There are many arrangements I must make once the Domanie gets to Sly Fox; he will have another translator to take him to the Falls while I travel west with the French. I will not see you soon again but I will arrange for you to come to me when the Acadians are leaving."

Leaving?

"This will happen when the early snows are deep enough. Armand will come to Boston to fetch you."

"I will?" Armand asked.

"You will."

Armand shrugged. "Very well."

Duval turned away, neither nodding to Dimock nor acknowledging him at all—nor her, an unimportant white woman. He trotted away in the ground-eating jog that Indians used when journeying.

"Where is he going?" the Reverend demanded. "Is he setting off on tribal errands?" he asked, answering his own question. "What did he say to you?"

"He thanked me for helping the Acadians," Armand said.

"Oh. I didn't hear him say that word, Acadian," Dimock objected. Was he suspicious?

"He calls them 'people of the earth'—meaning farmers. He would not use the French name—Acadian—because he is not French," Margaret explained.

Dimock nodded. "They do have ingenious ways of expressing themselves, the natives. Did you know that Massachusetts means 'great hill country'? Probably referring to the Blue Hills of Canton. And Pawtucket means 'where the river falls'. When we call it Pawtucket Falls, we are saying 'where the river falls falls!"

"Yes, it is a very direct speech. You would do well to respect that, sir."

"I do, I do!"

"And you would do well to respect the natives themselves."

"I do, I do!"

"You called that man 'boy'."

He reddened violently, making the flowing white hair around his face even whiter. "Gracious me! You're right. And since he speaks some English, he knew what I'd said. He gave no indication of it."

"He would not demean himself in such a way."

"You know a great deal about the natives, Miss Roberge."

"They accompanied us sometimes when I was in Acadia," she lied. "And the men took time to explain them when I'd notice something strange or different. Once when we were negotiating with them, they laid down on the ground full length in order to think about what we were offering."

He laughed. "How droll!"

But they also can be cruel, she did not add. Surely he knew it, and surely he needed no reminding. He was the Voice, crying in the Wilderness. God would protect him.

CHAPTER

12

December

"Ronald says this is hog-wash," exclaimed Clara Newcomb. She waved the single printed page about, as though it were a flag, and passed it on to Elizabeth Dyer. "Broadsides like this just appear in coffee houses and taverns and at the market, and they're free. A lot of commoners read them, and they're outrageous."

"I didn't know commoners could read," drawled Penelope Smythe, drawing her shawl closer as the winter wind howled beyond the window. "What does it say, this outrageous article?"

"Find out for yourself," said Madam Dyer said. "I'll give it to you when I'm finished."

"Don't be mean," Madam Smythe pouted. "Reading it is too much trouble."

"It praises the wisdom of relieving Governor Shirley of his position as Commander and Chief of the North American Army," Margaret told her.

"Oh, that. Anything else interesting?"

"It says that everyone here knows how inept the governor is, and that is why he has had so much trouble raising a militia to attack French forts out west."

Margaret Roberge-soon-to-be Blake knew things they did not know, and although they were trained not to care, with the presence of such a knowledgeable creature in their midst, they loved prying information out of her. They were reluctant to welcome her too warmly, for it was well known that she spent her days running Roberge Imports—unless Madam Blake could coax her away for a social hour or two, as she had today.

"Tea, Miss Margaret?" asked the maid Sofia, circulating among the ladies.

"Thank you."

"My Thomas believes these broadsides are treasonous," Mrs. Blake said. "Sofia, have more wood brought in, if you please. It's getting chilly."

"I must go home soon, Madam," Margaret said, and smiled with coy sweetness. "Robert is acalling this evening, and I would be ready for him."

"Ah! Ah! Ah!" they all chorused. Courting was such a fine thing!

"Sofia, see to it that the phaeton is made ready. But the rest of you can stay for a while, can you not?" Mrs. Blake asked her friends. "So it'll be worth building up the fire?"

They agreed.

"But do you think it's true, my dear?" she asked Margaret. "That these broadsides are treasonous?"

"I think it depends on what you believe is treason. The editorials always stop short of anything actionable."

"Not quite a denial, Miss Roberge," Caroline Cunningham interjected.

She chuckled. They pretended to be brainless, but they were clever enough.

"And this person? Do you know who he is?"

"I can guess," Margaret smiled. "But I'm more interested in getting him to write about the governor's treatment of the Acadians."

"Ah, the Acadians," they breathed. They all knew about her involvement with those hapless prisoners of war, and while they admired it, they did not wish to discuss it. It was fine to know which way the wind was blowing, but one did not have to go out-of-doors to find out.

Where, at that moment, snow-flakes were drifting down, just a small squall to add to the accumulation of early winter.

"Has anyone heard anything further about the Governor's new wife?" asked Derry Winslow—Desire, who had eschewed her Puritan background and her Puritan name when she married into the Upper Orders.

"Well, she's here. In Boston," Penelope told them. "Living in the North End."

"I think it's a little strange that His Excellency hasn't presented her."

"He hasn't been here, if you remember. He's been in charge of the army."

"Well, according to this broadside, he isn't in charge any more."

"Personally, I don't think he's even married to the woman."

"La!"

"His landlord's daughter, when he was in Paris? I wager he knocked her up."

Coarse language from a woman of the Better Sort. But their husbands weren't here to monitor, and they reveled in it.

"And had to marry her."

"Or at least hide her somewhere until the bastard could be born."

On and on they elaborated, their favorite indoor sport.

Margaret rose, and Mrs. Blake accompanied her. "Excuse us, girls, while I get my darling Margaret on her way."

"Of course, of course," they agreed, now having moved on to eviscerating the wife of one of His Excellency's counsel members.

Away from the fire, the foyer was distinctly chilly. The coachman waited there with her cloak, and prepared to escort her to the phaeton waiting outside.

"Please don't tarry, Madam," she urged Robert's mother. "It's too cold here. You'll be coming to Sunday dinner, am I correct?"

"Looking forward to it, my dear." Mrs. Blake kissed her cheek in farewell and hurried back to the receiving room and its warmth, while Margaret hurried into the phaeton and gratefully took the heated brick given her by the driver, to keep her hands warm.

Soon it would be too inclement to go over the Mystic Meadow with her Boston friends, the ones who had undertaken the Acadian Endeavour and collected the first items of donated clothing. After that they had collected warm clothes too, and often the whole group of them had gone with her to Mystic Meadow on day trips, when the Blakes could free up their men to serve as crew for *Robin*. There they helped the women sort through the clothing, and prepare the noon meal while practising their French.

Their determination was amusing, and the Acadians, understanding upon which side their bread was buttered, played along.

"*Bonjour*," they would call.

"Bone jure," the girls would answer. "Comment tallie voo?"

How Robert hated her on-going involvement with the prisoners. Hated her collecting clothes, taking her friends to

CHAPTER TWELVE

Mystic Meadow. And, of course, he hated her managing Roberge Imports.

"My dear," he asked stiffly when he had called last Wednesday. "Are you sure you're not overdoing it?"

"Over-doing what?" she asked, her voice deliberately vague and innocent.

"Well, this business thing, for one."

"Papa is much improved, Robert." This was untrue. "But he can't be left alone just yet."

"You are the one who runs the business, the one who is really in charge. This is socially unacceptable and you must know it. Continuing to collect clothing for the Acadians just makes it worse."

"Winter is coming," she pointed out. "Surely you've noticed."

"You needn't be sarcastic."

"And when I'm there, I can find out the progress of timber cutting. Your father wants to know if they are doing what they've promised to do. Surely you don't object to that!"

"Sometimes I think you go just to talk to that St. Martin fellow," Robert pouted. "Are you sure there's not more going on between the two of you than you're letting on?"

"Robert! Are you jealous of that poor, defeated farm boy?"

"You're more interested in him than you are in me. You won't even let me kiss you."

Surely it would not be much longer, and Robert must not be allowed to turn away—not yet.

"Perhaps I can see my way clear to doing something about that." She flipped open her fan and hid behind it. "Even though we are not yet betrothed. As long as you don't tell, sir!"

"Next Wednesday, perhaps?" The light of lust lit up his eyes. "6:00?" His usual visiting time.

"Very well."

He scooped her hand up and kissed it sloppily, like a hound grateful for a biscuit. "Wednesday," he panted.

"You have a visitor," Lucy told her as soon as she opened the door. "You may as well keep your cloak. He's in the shed."

A shiver, a thrill, chased itself through her. Was it time? She ran through the house, fleeing to the shed where Armand waited.

Armand.

He had never come here before. How did he even know which house was hers?

"*Bon soir, Mademoiselle*," he smiled. "Can you guess why I am here? The Acadians are departing Mystic Meadow tonight. You must come."

Tonight! So much was pending at Roberge Imports, a new shipment due soon, new clerks to train whom she had hired to help Lucy run the shop in her absence. And Lucy. She must be told everything. . . .

"A heavy storm approaches," Armand said. "I came here upon the Charlestown Ferry; its man says he can return at midnight. The tide, it will have turned by then."

Tonight. She would talk to Lucy, bid Papa farewell—though how could she do it without bursting into tears?

And then there was Robert, who was due for his promised visit within the hour.

"You cannot wait out here, my friend," she told him. "You must come inside."

"Someone might see me."

"Worry not. We have a pantry in which you can hide. Come!"

She took his hand and led him to shelter, and warmth, and a meal.

CHAPTER TWELVE

"I hope you all are finished with your supper!" Robert cried, slinging his cloak onto the front hall rack. "I should hate to incommode you. How are you, sir?" he asked Papa, who clearly could not remember who he was, but stirred as though to rise in greeting. "Oh, please, sir, do not disturb yourself! With your permission, sir, it's Miss Margaret I've come to see."

"Margaret!" Papa exclaimed, as though Robert's visit were an entirely unexpected event instead of one that had been happening every week since August. He had entirely forgotten the motive for these calls. "Oh, yes! Margaret! By all means, sir." Helplessly, he turned to Lucy. "It's tea time, isn't it? Shouldn't we serve the gentleman some tea?"

"If you like, Uncle. I'll get it ready."

"I'll come with you."

They linked arms and started for the pantry.

The pantry!

"Why not just take Papa upstairs and read to him," Margaret interposed swiftly. Turning to Robert, she said, "We keep extra logs and kindling up there, so he will be comfortable when it's chilly, as it is tonight."

"Would you enjoy that, Uncle?" Lucy asked. "We're in the middle of Pilgrim's Progress," she told Robert. "Are you familiar with it?"

"No," he answered, no doubt hoping his brevity would get rid of them the sooner.

"We're about ready for the Delectable Mountains."

"Oh, yes," Papa crowed. "The next stage of the Christian Journey. Perhaps you are Anglican, Mr. Blake. We dissenters love Pilgrim's Progress, but the Church of England is less enthusiastic."

Margaret kissed Papa's cheek. "I'll check in with you before I go to bed, darling Father."

"If I'm not awake, I wish you well, my darling." He looked her full in the face, searching. Did he know? Could he hear it in her voice? "*Adieu*," he murmured. "*Adieu*." Go with God.

She nearly lost control then and there, watching Lucy lead him away. Turning to her suitor, she made herself smile. Now was the time. "I apologize for the delay."

"Quite all right." He waved the inconvenience away, as though swatting at flies.

"Will you be seated?" She led him into the parlor, indicating that he might take one of the settees. "Perhaps you'd like a spot of wine?"

"Yes, indeed." His voice was soothing, as though he expected her to be nervous over the promised kiss.

"I'll fetch two glasses, and a decanter." Which would be in the pantry, she remembered.

The pantry!

"I think we have some Madeira," she said loudly, so that Armand would hear and be warned. She fetched the wine goblets from the dining room cabinet, set them on a small table by the settee. Taking a candle and lighting it from the sconce by the mantle, she hastened back and opened the pantry door, adjacent to the kitchen. Held the light high. Armand was waiting at the pickle barrel, knife in hand. He nodded when she put her finger to her lips in a shushing gesture, slipped his knife back inside his boot and handed her the Madeira when she pointed at it.

"Ah!" If he were impatient with her lack of preparation, Robert did not show it. He took the bottle from her. "Let us see what we have here. Madiera? Lovely." He poured two glasses, offered one to her, leaned back on the settee and crossed one leg over the other, as if he owned the place. "To us," he offered in toast, then slowly emptied his glass.

Waiting, he watched as she steadily sipped hers. The room was suddenly warmer and more friendly than it had been.

When her goblet was empty, he quickly poured another. "To our friendship."

Again they drank, a little faster this time, the room tipping a bit as they did so.

This won't be so hard, she thought. I can hardly feel a thing.

He poured a third glass, this one for her, and sat back a little, the better to watch her. "Do you know what I think?"

"No," she shook her head carefully, so that the walls would not spin around her.

"I think you ought to allow me to touch your breast first. Before I kiss you."

"Sir!" she threw her free arm across her chest, splashing the wine on her bodice.

"Just give it a try." He leaned toward her and pushed her arm down toward her lap, laid his other hand on her breast. The heat penetrated through the cool wine and on through to her chemise. "Like that."

She looked deeply into his eyes—which she had not ever done before—and saw something in them that she could not identify or put a label to. It was urgent, and she was not sure it was nice.

The balance had shifted somehow. Until this moment she had always had control. It was he who implored, who panted, who prostrated himself that she might yield a token of her favor and esteem. He was not imploring now, nor prostrating himself either.

He squeezed softly, kneading, then took the wine glass from her free hand. "I think you said something about a kiss?"

Relinquishing her bosom, he raised his hands up to the base of her throat, to her ears, and then positioned her chin so that he could press his lips firmly on hers and pry her mouth open with his insistent tongue, thrusting it in deep. Deep as it would go and leaving it there, inert.

She clawed at his fingers and loosened them, pulled away. "I can't breathe," she gasped, nearly gagging.

"I should not have let it go on so long," he admitted. "I am sorry. But you are so delectable, my dear. All parts of me think so. See?"

He gestured toward his crotch, where his erection had caused a straining lump to press against the drop-down panel of his breeches.

"Oh!" she whispered, as though overcome with admiration. "Oh, my! May I?" Without waiting for a reply, she lightly put her hand on the lump. "Permit me to return the favor."

Gently, she squeezed, much as he had squeezed her breast.

"Oh!" He gasped and shivered and threw his head back with an agonized mewling, and she knew what had happened.

The room was quiet; on the hearth the fire snapped, a coal lit up, subsided. She put her head on his shoulder as though in satisfaction, and he sighed, as though indeed, his cup ran over. And another sigh. Or was it a deep breath? And another....

Softly, Robert snored.

The situation had been resolved.

The room spun as she staggered to her feet. "I'll be right back," she whispered, in case he could hear, and tiptoed away. When he woke up, Robert would most likely find that the front of his breeches was stained. He might need the proverbial fig leaf to cover it. Supporting herself on one piece of furniture and then another, she moved to the front of the house, returned with his cloak and threw it at him.

CHAPTER TWELVE

"Umph!" he exclaimed, raising his head and looking around.

"It's time for you to leave, my dear. I've brought your cloak." The room had stopped moving; she took the wine bottle and glasses into the kitchen, giving him time to cover himself and a chance, on her part, to regain a measure of sobriety. When she returned he was standing by the front door, trying not to look sheepish, she thought, but she gave him no time to speculate about his dignity. Reaching up to pat his cheek, she opened the door, and stepped back.

"Until another time," she murmured with the smallest of curtseys. He took her hand, bowed over it, and left without meeting her eyes.

Left! He was gone, and she would never have to endure him again! She locked the door, lit another candle before extinguishing the parlor lamps.

She released Armand from the pantry and established him at the kitchen hearth with a loaf of bread and a jug of hard cider. Quietly she climbed the stairs to speak with Lucy about the things she had not yet told her and what the future might—or might not—hold for them both.

Very soon.

CHAPTER

13

The Escape

The ferry had been waiting, as promised. The tide had barely turned; the night held neither stars nor moon, so dark that the stern of the boat could not be discerned from the bow. The drifting snowflakes were falling more heavily now as Margaret and Armand huddled, wrapped in a rough horse blanket supplied by the ferry tender.

When they arrived at Mystic Meadow, the scene was one of controlled chaos. The Acadians, man, woman, and child, were assembled at the back of the house, dressed in their warmest donated clothing. Numerous Mi'kmaqs were helping fasten snowshoes to their boots.

"They have been making the snowshoes all fall," Armand told her. "There is a pair for you, and some quilted clothing for travel and a fur robe to keep you warm when you are resting."

"Snowshoes! I've never used them, Armand!"

"It will be easy. I will show you how, and the path will be already beaten down by the others, because we will be following them."

"How far will the Acadians go? Where will they be taken?"

"To Quebec."

"Armand! I cannot walk to Quebec!"

"You may not need to, *Mademoiselle*. I know not what Marc plans."

"Where is he?"

"I hope we will see him at the camp of Sly Fox, which is as far as we will travel tonight."

"How long will it take?"

"We will probably be there by dawn."

Dawn—which, now in December, was many hours away. But when it came! Then she would lose herself in the embrace of the one for whose sake she would give up everything in her world. She would very likely speak French for the rest of her life, and she would be surrounded by the enemies of King George, her sovereign, and of Boston, her home. She had given up Papa and Lucy and her inheritance ...

These thoughts must be banished. Leaving the known for the unknown was never accomplished easily, she was sure. "Armand, I do not mean to complain. I thank you for your help."

"And the Acadians, *Mademoiselle*, thank you for yours!"

As indeed they did, greeting her as she and Armand arrived.

"*Il est l'oiseau chanteur!*" It is the Singing Bird!

"*La femme merveilleux est venu!*" The wonderful woman has come!

"*Mademoiselle, tu es manifique!*"

Once in the back garden, she, too, put on donated clothing: a quilted coat, breeches made small, just for her, that tucked into boots of thick hide laced up to the knee; a scarf to protect her ears.

The Acadians were hustled away; now Margaret and Armand were alone.

Tying her parcel and a fur robe into a small, soft bundle he could carry on his back, he explained, "You will not need the robe when you are travelling. You will be very hot! But when you stop for resting, then the fur keeps you warm until you are ready to move on. And now, *Mademoiselle*, we will practice."

The snowshoe frames were tied onto her boots with leather thongs. When they had been saplings, three months ago, they had been bent and twisted into the necessary shape and when sufficiently dried, webbed with narrow strips of leather.

Taking her arm and tucking it inside his own, he explained, "You will step forward, as far as you can. A long step. A giant step." He pulled her forward so that her right foot was well ahead of the left. "This is necessary so you do not step on the opposite snowshoe. If you do, you will fall instantly." He stood away, holding her hand. "Now bring the left foot far enough forward so you are not stepping on the right snowshoe." He balanced her as she awkwardly complied.

"Again."

Another two giant steps were taken.

"Now, try it by yourself."

He let go, and she fell over sideways, unable to rise without his help.

"This does not seem to be working, Armand."

"But it will when you—what is the word for *prendre de grands orogres . . .*"

"Strides. Take big strides."

"Just so! Thus your own body's motion carries the snow shoe forward, not just the leg moving. You must stride with vigor, *Mademoiselle*."

Unaccustomed as she was to striding, which a woman in layers of petticoats could not do, she tried it and went several yards before toppling over. Hauling her up, Armand exclaimed, "You do well! Try again."

Again she moved, lunging as he instructed.

"Bend at the knee, bend more low, or you will strain your legs."

She had already discovered the truth of this. "When you are moving, fast, the snow shoes will take care of themselves, and will remain facing in the proper direction," Armand explained. "But you must move with a will, *Mademoiselle*. No strolling. You will follow me; I will stop often to wait for you. Do not call out. We know not who might be near. This is British territory."

With the trail already trampled down, and with freedom afforded by the leggings, lunging rapidly became rhythmic. Exhilarated, flying more freely than she had ever done, Margaret raced along the path until her labored breathing forced a stop. In time, Armand came back.

"I wondered, *Mademoiselle*, how long you could keep that pace."

She could only gasp in response.

"Perhaps, when we resume, you will not go so far before resting. Going fast is well, but not so much distance at one time."

"*Tres bien*," she panted.

And so there were many rests.

On through the night they travelled, the snow falling heavily now, until her legs simply gave out. Trembling, they refused to move.

"Be of good heart," Armand encouraged, patting her shoulder. "You have done well. We are not far from Sly Fox's camp. I will carry you the rest of the way." Removing her snowshoes, he wrapped her in the fur robe, then squatted. She put her arms around his neck, leaning against him as he rose, and wrapped her legs around his waist. Picking up her personal pack and snowshoes, he moved forward in a stride much faster than hers.

"It is very beautiful, the forest, in the dark. And very quiet," she said softly into his ear.

"Always quiet in snow falling. But voices carry. Best not to speak."

Despite his great strength, he was breathing heavily.

"Just tell me how much time it will take."

"*Une heure.* An hour," he said with confidence. "Just enjoy."

And she did. Loosening the robe from around her throat, she relished the inpouring of cold air on her hot skin, and lifted her sweaty face to the downfalling snow. Then bundling up until she again grew too hot and then uncovering again, to become part of the forest, part of the night. They were alone, alone, alone out here—wherever 'here' was. Probably Indians followed, unheard, and no doubt several ran ahead, but never did she see one, and certainly heard nothing.

Then the trees became silhouetted, and the sky became gray, and then grew much lighter than the trees, and then there was a wide swath of beaten down snow, and then it appeared—the camp of Sly Fox. The Acadians had passed through several hours ago, and from the looks of it, the Indians had not returned to their shelters, but instead had waited for Armand around a central fire. It was surrounded by many watu's, some elongated, some more modest, some small, no doubt for storage. Children wandered here and there, with no one appearing to think they ought to be asleep. Many of the men were drinking out of wine-skins, the women continually refilled containers of something that looked like porridge, placed on stones at the edges of the central blaze.

A welcoming clamor arose as Armand squatted to let her slide off his back. Promptly she collapsed. Laughing and pointing, the women came forward to help her onto to her feet, pulling her toward one of the watu's.

It was a little larger than the smallest ones, as though it had held a single family. Near the doorway were several window openings, covered now. On the other side of the doorway was a stack of stiff, untanned hides. Several sleeping mats and robes were rolled up neatly at the back wall. In the center a low fire was banked, with some kindling. As many people as could, crowded into the watu behind the head woman.

"This is the wife of Sly Fox. She leads when the men are gone," Armand explained from the doorway, surrounded by all the others who could not fit inside. "Her name is Crow Flying. She knows only a little French. She will make sure the women check up on you from time to time, bring you food and water, if you wish it, build up the fire if you need them to. You will stay here until Duval comes for you. Here is your pack."

She reached to take it, but the women snatched it away and opened it.

One held up the bathing sponge.

"Eeeee," they approved, nodding.

Her monthly wadding was displayed.

"Aahaa," they remarked knowledgeably.

Her sleeveless tunic.

"Aeee."

Blue Blanket.

"Yeeaa."

Once it had all been examined, including the breech clout—"Hmmm"—they stuffed everything back in.

Crow Flying, held out her hands.

"*Bien . . . ven . . . nue.*"

"It's about the only French she knows," Armand explained. "But she is more than willing to take you under her wing, since you are Marc's woman."

"*Merci beaucoup,*" Margaret said carefully and clearly. The sparkle in the old woman's eyes told her that there were a few other words known, among them 'thank you very much'. "Please tell her that now I wish only to sleep."

He did so. The women built up the fire, put her pack on the stack of hides by the door, spread out a mat and a sleeping robe for her use, then left.

"I think you will be fine here. I wish to tell you that I am pleased to see the blue blanket again!"

She smiled with tears of gratitude in her eyes. Ducking his head in acknowledgement, he covered the doorway with a deer skin and she was left in the dimness of the shrouded hut.

Snow fell and fell. Despite having not slept, she was too excited to do so now. The women looked in periodically, building up the fire and leaving both unappetizing food, wrapped in dried corn husks, and water in hollowed out gourds. After much consultation with Crow Flying, they also brought a full wine-skin such as those from which the men had been drinking.

She sipped at the edge of a gourd. The water tasted like squash. Perhaps, if she added wine from the skin, it would give the water a better taste. She dribbled a little in.

Odd flavor, but curiously warming. And the taste of squash was gone. She sipped some more, took up the other gourd and flavored its water, reached under the deer-skin door and put snow into the first gourd and left it near the fire to melt. They were small, the gourds, and she mixed many more portions, finishing one, then the other, then another.

The day floated by. The snow stopped. Feet ran by her hut, followed by the cries of children. She peeked around the edge of the door. They were chasing a ball of twine—no doubt a vine in its earlier life—batting it about with sticks, racing from one end of the village to the other, trying to beat one another to the next stroke. There were no women to be seen.

They must be gathered inside one of the larger watu's, for now that her own watu door was open, she could hear their gabbling. Probably doing whatever women did in the winter—pounding acorns into meal or pelts into softness, talking together amiably as they worked. When she dropped the doorway pelt, their chatter was only a murmur which she had not picked up on before. Or, perhaps, they had just started.

She poked a stick into her little fire, picked up a piece of pemmican and broke off a small chunk, though she was far from hungry. In fact she was bored. It might be a long time before Marc arrived, she realized. If he took much longer, her only recourse would be to continue drinking joy juice from the wine- skin—but it was nearly empty. Empty!

How could that be!

Some women came by and removed the window coverings so that light could enter. Then someone brought in more pemmican and another wineskin. Ah! They had provided a way to make the slow march of time pleasant! And now that the watu was lighter, she was able to see more than she had before. She could explore.

Finishing up the contents of the nearly depleted wine-skin, she sampled the new one—ah, yes, it was good—and crawled over to the sleeping robes and mats at the back of the shelter, looked them over carefully. A corn husk doll wrapped up in a scrap of red wool was tucked in between robes. No doubt the cloth was obtained from a bolt traded for a fur. Now a little girl had a blanket for her dolly. Margaret smiled in woozy benevolence, went back to her own mat and robe, tipped up the wine skin for another sip, and decided to explore further.

Three iron pots were lined up beside the sleeping robes. She examined them. Dusky red. The women should know that iron pots required a coating of fat to keep them from rusting. But she could not speak to them about it. Perhaps when Armand come back with Marc....

She returned to her fire, built it up, sipped again.

On the pile of hides by the door opening was her pack. What had she brought with her? A sponge. The women seemed impressed with it. Sooner or later she must use it. Surely her face was dirty! Perhaps now? From beneath the deerskin door she scooped up some snow and rubbed it on her cheeks, chin, and forehead.

Headache.

Snow too cold. She dug into the pack and found Armand's blue blanket, dried her face with it, pressed her hands to her forehead and tried to warm her head up. The pounding eased.

Another helping of joy juice, and she was as good as new. Then saw that above the pile of hides a mirror was attached to the rough wall. Exploring further, she found that underneath the pelts was a small-ish box, just the right size to sit upon when the lady of the house wished to improve her appearance. She would be able to see herself in the mirror, and use red powder on her cheeks and cause them to glow. Indigo—just a trace—on her eye lids, and a piece of pointed charcoal to enhance her eyebrows. Pushing the pelts to one side, Margaret seated herself on the box and looked in the mirror. Awful! Pale and pasty. She could benefit from the impliments of beauty that she had imagined would be in the box! It was important to look her best when Marc arrived!

She slid off the box and lifted the lid to look.

Within, on a length of neatly folded burlap exactly the size of the box's interior, was a comb, and beads strung on a sinew to form a necklace, small pots of powered color, and the covers of John Eliot's Bible: **Wunneenupanatamwe Up Biblum God.**

She stared at it. Touched it, to be sure it was real. Where were the pages?

Perhaps inside.

And the necklace. Were these the kind of beads that Dimock had brought with him? One bead was much the same as the next, was it not? Perhaps the husband of the watu's little family had bought them for his wife when he last traded with a white man. They could have come from anywhere. A bead was a bead, was it not?

She took up the Bible's covers and put them on the floor, wound the bead necklace around her wrist, so it became a bracelet, and rolled the little paint pots up in the burlap, and looked into the shadowed interior—

The opening at the windows let in enough light to see a collection of scalps. A blonde one, a tiny red one, several brown and black ones, and a white one, luxuriant, with a long tail tied with black grosgrain ribbon.

She went cold, cold all over, and numb, numb all over, and the hut began to spin, became darker, and darker yet as she closed her eyes and curled up by the box, curled into a small ball, as small as she could get, and went elsewhere, far, far from this place and the horror it hid.

She could hear the voices of women as they came near the watu. The babble quieted as two of them entered and someone leaned over her, put a hand on her forehead. One left and brought two more, and they gently unfolded her, straightened her out on her mat and robe by the fire. A lengthy discussion ensued. She could hear it all, and if she opened her eyes, no doubt she would be able to see the speakers, but she was too far away to care.

Crow Flying's voice took over; everyone instantly quieted, then someone left and soon returned with yet another person, malodorous, voice a croak. Likely very, very old.

A drum had been brought into the watu. A resonance from deep within it set the very air atremble. Outside, rattles must have been distributed among the women, who encircled the watu and rattled an accompaniment, on and off. Occasionally the old person sang a whining petition. Nearby the village dogs threw back their heads and howled, long, lonely moaning and without wanting to, Margaret returned to the present from which she had fled.

Sitting up, her head splitting, she vomited into the fire. Hissing, sizzling, it flickered out. The hut dimmed. The drum stopped. One by one the rattles were made to be still.

"Water," she moaned. "*S'il vous plait.* Water."

More gourds were brought.

The sullied fire was shoveled up and taken away, a new one started. The rattles were returned to wherever they were stored, and the women went back to the big watu to resume their work, this time silently. Someone helped the medicine person back to wherever she or he and the drum resided. Crow Flying restored the burlap mat and the paint pots and the Bible covers to the box, closed its lid, stacked the pelts up again. Then she stood outside the doorway, waiting.

Rocking back and forth on her sleeping robe, eyes closed, arms crossed tightly, hugging herself, Margaret did not know how long she, too, waited. It did not matter. In time, Crow Flying and Marc were talking outside, her harsh voice and his quiet one discussing the affair in the watu. Crow Flying went away and Marc entered, sat down beside her. She did not look at him, continued to rock.

He spoke softly. "Crow Flying tells me that Old Crooked Stick brought your soul back from the dead."

She rocked.

"Crow Flying said you were without power to move or speak."

"Yes," she said finally.

"So clearly something was wrong with your body's soul. If it had continued in the direction it was headed, you would have crossed the abyss into the realm of death. But your spirit soul heard the drum, listened to the women surrounding the watu, heard the song of Crooked Stick, and brought your body soul back."

She said nothing, rocking, rocking.

He did not attempt to stop her. Resting his elbows on his knees, he studied her closely, now that his eyes were accustomed to the dimness, and the silence between them became unbearable.

"I got drunk."

"So it would seem." His tone was soothing, as if he were speaking to a child.

"Did they mean to? Get me drunk, I mean?"

"I think they were being hospitable. They save alcohol for very special occasions. They must have thought this was one of them."

She rocked.

"Tell me what happened."

She thought of the words she must use, and could not.

"Come, Little Singing Bird, how is it that you were rolled up into a ball, like a frightened porcupine?" he asked gently, but persistently. "Crow Flying says that's the way they found you."

She took a shaking deep breath. "Have you seen—do you know—what is in yonder box?"

"I do now."

She looked at him, finally.

"This is not my village," he reminded her. "I have never been in this watu before. And so I did not know anything about the box."

"Did you look inside?" A long silence enfolded them. She poured a little water from a gourd onto the fire, where it spat and sent up unpleasant-smelling smoke. "If you had looked, you would find the covers of a New Testament printed in the Algonquian language."

CHAPTER THIRTEEN

He said nothing. His eyes were steady.

"I know of only one man who had such a book. You know of only one, also."

He only watched.

"I looked." Her eyes filled, and now it returned—the great sorrow that had locked her in its embrace from the time she'd opened the box to this unbearable moment.

"There are scalps in there. I saw one I recognized," she forced herself on, through her pain and the heaviness of her guilt. "It was white, and thick, and wavy and tied with a black ribbon. I have seen only one man with such a head of hair."

Silence.

He drew a deep breath. "Dimock was here when I saw him last. I left him and went on to meet the headmen of other villages to the west. And to find, if I could, someone who would translate for him and teach him to speak the language."

"You left him here, unable to communicate."

"The governor, Shirley, was preparing an attack on Fort Niagara. There were men who depended on me to tell them of this."

Her voice came from a place within herself that she had never known of before. "Have you helped Indians kill settlers and burn their crops and houses and carry off their women and children, those they do not murder?" Her mind was clear now, like water running over stones, bringing out their color and richness. "I must know if you are only engaged in defeating the British army at their forts, Marc, or if you are also waging war against the western settlements—against the Americans."

"You do not need to know! Marguerite! You do not!" He had turned to face her now.

"You are wrong," she told him. "I do need to know. I am no longer innocent. Beloved, if your joining with the Indians means that more

Americans—farmers and their wives and their children—will die, I must know it so I can decide what to do. And Dimock! Did you know they would kill him? Did you talk it over with them?"

"I did not. I told them he was to be taken to the Falls, that he wished to continue John Eliot's work, and if they could not find anyone, I would take him myself when I was finished with my work at the Western Forts."

"Did you come back?"

"Yes."

"And?"

"He was dead already." Duval's voice became low, very low and his sorrow and anger filled the watu like a gathering storm that would end the world as they knew it. "They betrayed my trust."

Let it not be true, Lord, she implored. Please, let it not be true. "Marc—did they—"

"Yes."

A great emptiness was filling her, one she could not turn away from, but must face. The sacred beliefs she had inherited throughout her life towered above her, implacable, immovable. She had played a part in Dimock's terrible death, and by leaving him here, Marc had played a part, too.

"Marguerite," he said at last, "they saw him as one more Congregational minister who would lure the Red Man into the snare of the English. A man who would corrupt the souls of the Indians with tales of the Son of God, and His insistence that they turn the other cheek and wear English clothes and sign meaningless peace treaties. I am not followed here as I am in Acadia. My request was not honored. I am sorry—more sorry than I can say—but I cannot blame them."

"Do you mean that? You really do not blame them?"

"Do you know how many tribes have lost their hunting lands already? If the English have their way, they will do to us what the French King Louis did to your people, the Huguenots. Are you unable to understand that we will not allow it to happen to us?"

"It's not something I can debate with you, Marc. But I would know if you, yourself, have ever subjected a helpless captive to ritual torture."

"I have not. I would not. But I respect the right of my brothers to do it. This is how they avenge injustice. The spirits of the dead are appeased and their own rage is assuaged."

He stood in a single liquid motion, reached for her hand and pulled her to her feet. "You must make a choice, my sweet Singing Bird. It is a blood choice, a life and death choice. It is a cruel choice, and you must make it."

She looked deeply into his eyes. "Beloved, if I asked you to come south with me—to a colony far away—to Maryland or Virginia, and start your life over with a new, anglicized name, leave your people behind—right now—this day—would you do it? For my sake?"

He did not answer. The forest was silent. The sun was setting now; the nearby stream flowed quiet beneath its ice. Nothing was the same. Nothing would ever be the same.

A baby cried, was comforted.

"I don't care if you kill English soldiers," she said finally, taking a step back. "They are paid for their risk. I don't even care if you kill militia. They would kill you if they could. But I care if you kill men who carry pitchforks instead of guns. I care if you kill women and children and destroy their homes and their hopes."

His fists were clenched, and there was sweat on his brow. "They killed everyone in my mother's village, women and children and old men. They spared no one, and burnt their bodies so we could not bury them and return to bring food for their spirits and tokens of our remembrance. Why should I care if a few English people are killed now?"

He stopped. Watched her. His eyes changed, somehow; a decision was being reached somewhere deep within himself, in a place she could not enter, and he was quiet for a long while.

"I told you I am sorry about the Domanie," he said at last. "When you think of me, remember that." He reached out. "I must return you to your own people, my Singing Bird. Your feelings do you credit. You, like me, have limits, boundaries that you cannot transgress. Most women I have known would not care, but you are not like most women I have known."

He pulled her to him, her body in his arms so close, so much a part of his body, that for that moment they were as one, and he kissed her, long and deep and gut-wrenching, and then put her from him, his shoulders straight. "Armand will take you back to Boston."

She did not try to stop him as he left her, went out of the watu and somewhere into the camp. A squaw brought her some supper and built up the fire. She ate what she could, to keep up her strength. Knowing she would not sleep, she lay down on the robe and pulled another up around her ears. Around and through and beneath her consciousness the facts rolled here and there like a marble on a plate, no longer arousing guilt or disappointment or dismay but refusing to settle and leave her in peace.

In some part of her mind, or in some place in her heart, there would never be peace again. She knew too much.

❧

The night crept by. The trees separated themselves from the sky. By morning Armand and Yves were waiting by the fire. The tribe waited also, silently watching when she came out of the hut, carrying her pack.

She looked around for Marc, but he was gone.

Gone, as she'd known he would be.

CHAPTER THIRTEEN

This man she had loved so well—loved still—this man who could set her loins throbbing with a well-measured glance—this man for whom she would have given up her way of life—everything she had known—this man did not stay to witness her departure. Or would not. Or could not. Just as he had not or could not before, in Acadia, at Fort Lawrence.

She stepped into her snowshoes and Armand bound them to her boots, gave Yves her pack. Nodding to Crow Flying, she took her place between the men.

The woods was filled with bleakness, laced with bare branches, the pines dark, and the sky sullen, perhaps waiting for more snow.

Her stiffened legs warmed as she took up the rhythm of the lunging stride, as though she'd always hiked thus on snow. As she paced, left side, then right, then left, her mind which last night could not think at all, now refused to stop.

She had not known that within herself was an unbreachable limit, that would bring her to this juncture. She knew only that it was present now, an endlessly high battlement, unmovable, unshakeable, leaving her no room to maneuver nor any further decision to make. She did not deserve admiration for this boundary that had cost her the man she loved; she had not created it. It was simply there, and because of it she could let Marc Duval walk away from her, and she could walk away from him.

She could live with that knowledge and because of it she could cast her thoughts into a future without him, a future that would reveal other limits—hopefully gentler ones—that would unexpectedly define her.

They stopped and rested, ate some venison strips by a stream crusted with ice. Armand broke through to the water beneath and set her pack down for her to kneel upon and drink, helped her back up with a sad smile that told her he knew—

knew everything. Unwinding the bead necklace that was still twined around her wrist, she held it out to him. "It's all I have to give you, dear friend. Take it with my thanks."

He cupped it gently. "I will treasure it," he murmured. "*Merci.*"

They set off again.

Her mind resumed its pursuit of the future.

She would not marry Robert Blake, even if he agreed to relinquish coverture. She would not allow him to touch her. She distained him and always would.

She would continue to operate Roberge Imports with Papa, who would never know that she had left Boston. One day he would pass on and she would be the sole owner, and Lucy would be second in command, if that was her wish.

The income from Roberge, once Papa and Lucy were taken care of, could be used to help Tyler Moore buy Wagner Printing from the widow Wagner, and if his goal were still to publish the writing of the traitor Samuel Adams, she would support that belief. Adams, at least, was not impressed with wealth, and would stand firm for the common man. There was nothing wrong with that! Time would determine whether his beliefs would lead him to betray his king.

And if Tyler loved her yet, despite everything he knew about her, perhaps he would marry her one day and with him she could raise children who respected people different from themselves, children whom she could help to find where their own boundaries lay when the time came to stand up for what they believed was right. And maybe she would have a daughter whom she could teach how to run a business and keep it safe from the encroachment of a husband.

One day.

CHAPTER THIRTEEN

Somehow, she would grow past her memory of Marc Duval and her love for him. Somehow she would relinquish the freedom he had shown her, remembering it, cherishing it, perhaps, when a small bird sang to her in the spring sunshine, or a soft breeze brushed her cheek in summer, or the Red Leaf moon rose in October.

She would search out the Acadian refugees that would be scattered in villages and towns across Massachusetts, and she would speak their language with them and share their memories of a home lost and help them become American, if that was their wish.

And she would sing again, and perhaps even be happy....

One day....

Made in the USA
Charleston, SC
13 February 2017